Baby Shoes Copy

A Mt. Hope Southern Adventure Book Four

Lynne Gentry

Travel Light Press

Baby Shoes (Mt. Hope Southern Adventures, Book Four)

Copyright © 2017 by Lynne Gentry

Cover photo © 2017 Lynne Gentry

Cover Design by Lynne Gentry

Edited by Gina Calvert

ISBN: 978-09986412-3-2

Sign up for Lynne Gentry's Readers Club

and get the latest news on new releases and limited offers.

Details can be found at the end of **BABY SHOES**.

Summary

When the life you save is your own.

Madison Harper is an uptight doctor
on her way to international recognition.
Parker Kemp is no longer the fun-loving cowboy
Madison ignored in high school.
Parker's a humanitarian
who came home from a third-world country
with a life-threatening illness and an adorable daughter.
Maddie and Parker can't fall in love
if they're going to continue to save the world…or can they?

Opposites attract and bridges are mended
in the next heartwarming installment of the Harper family saga.

**Fast-paced humor. Tear-jerking candor.
Heart-melting romance.**

www.lynnegentry.com

Also By Lynne Gentry

MT. HOPE SOUTHERN ADVENTURES
Walking Shoes
Shoes to Fill
Dancing Shoes
Baby Shoes
Santa Shoes

WOMEN OF FOSSIL RIDGE SERIES
Flying Fossils
Finally Free
First Frost

MECIAL THRILLER
Murder on Flight 91
Ghost Heart
Port of Origin
Lethal Outbreak
Death Triangle

HISTORICAL/TIME TRAVEL

The Carthage Chronicles

For Megan

You are your mother's daughter.

CHAPTER ONE

The black convertible had been riding her bumper like the dread of her reluctant homecoming. Maddie glanced in the rearview and thumped the brakes as a back-off warning. The BMW sped to within reading distance of his front license plate.

Texas.

No self-respecting cowboy would be caught dead in such a useless off-road vehicle. Obviously, this jerk was not from this godforsaken stretch of pumpjacks, wind turbines, and scrub brush.

Sunset's crimson rays glinted off the dark glasses of the BMW's driver. He flashed a cocky smile and Maddie realized she'd been staring. She quickly averted her gaze back to the highway. If this upscale tailgater wasn't going to pass her on this empty stretch of interstate, he could eat her dust.

Maddie gripped the wheel of her new red sports car. The high-performance Porsche was the first splurge she'd allowed herself since receiving her share of the surprising fortune her father had left the family. Spending what her daddy had worked so hard to save on anything other than her education didn't seem right…at least not until she was gainfully employed. How she wished she could tell him about her new job…well, it wasn't her job yet, but she felt confident it would be.

According to the email she'd received from the head of the CDC's Disaster Epidemiology Department, they were reviewing her written argument for the hiring of more MDs than PhDs. After all, the agency claimed, they were as committed to alleviating human suffering as they were to disease containment during major international outbreaks of cholera or typhoid. The hiring committee agreed that her proposal to send doctors with epidemiology credentials along with a control scientist would put more effective boots on the ground. They went on to say that none of the other candidates had thought to add such an impressive and well-researched component to their application. Until all applicants could be interviewed, they would appreciate the opportunity to be the first to counter the many employment offers she was certain to receive.

Much as Maddie hated to credit her mother with any part of the CDC's positive response to the years of her own hard work, she'd learned the art of going the extra mile to make a good first impression from Momma.

Maddie pulled the band from her thick ponytail and shook her curls free. The time had come to see how far she could take herself. Her sandal barely tapped the gas and the speedometer instantly ticked up from 75 to 100 mph.

Golden strands whipping around her face, Maddie sailed past leaning fence posts and spindly mesquites. A brief glance in the mirror brought a smug smile to her face. No convertible. No surprise there.

Her gaze darted back to the highway. In the distance, Mt. Hope's billboard-sized exit sign stood like a flyswatter ready to smack her flat. She didn't need 20/20 vision to read the embarrassing slogan. Every Mt. Hope student was expected to recite the motto daily, right after the Texas pledge. After all, who wouldn't want to live in a place where "*Folks are more generous than the dust?*"

Her. That's who.

Something shiny flashed in Maddie's periphery. The BMW had caught her and was now humming alongside her Porsche. The tanned guy behind the leather-wrapped wheel delivered a challenging, game-on nod then zipped ahead.

"You don't mess with Texas, and you don't mess with me, mister," she mumbled between clenched teeth.

The desire to win had garnered Maddie a spot in one of the nation's toughest medical schools, followed by a prestigious residency match and, finally, acceptance into one of the top-ranking infectious disease fellowships.

Shaking this tailgater would be good practice for what lay ahead. If she had any hope of escaping her mother's plans to stuff her into a tidy box, she'd need more than a lead foot. She'd need a bucket-load of courage.

Maddie jammed the accelerator pedal to the floor. Her Porsche easily caught and passed the irritating car.

Thrilled that her drag racing skills had not atrophied during her years of riding crowded, northeastern subways, Maddie sped toward Mt. Hope's hideous exit sign. A split second before her planned veer toward the small town, the stalker car rocketed around. Bumpers almost kissing, she swerved toward the ditch as he cut her off. Maddie swerved back onto the road, laid on the horn, and gave the reckless guy behind the wheel the universal symbol of disapproval.

He pumped a victory fist in response.

She eased off the gas. Getting caught at the red light and being forced to stare at the back of this guy's pompous head was the last thing she needed today. Luckily, the speed racer treated the stoplight like a yield sign, slowing just long enough to throw her a triumphant wave through his open top. He peeled left and disappeared in the direction of Mt. Hope's small county hospital, the tiny medical facility Momma was always going on and on about, as if adding the second floor to the aging facility had suddenly transformed it into a premier healing destination.

Maddie coasted to a stop at the intersection, her knuckles white and jaw still clenched. The light turned green. Then yellow. Then red. Then green again. She couldn't make herself press the accelerator. Instead, she sat at the deserted intersection, car idling, hands sweating beneath her killer grip on the wheel. She had nearly been killed by a hot guy in a hot car. But she'd be lying to herself if she said that near-death experience was the reason her foot remained firmly on the brake.

Native scents of dust and cattle blew through the open window and cleared Maddie's nostrils of the last traces of city smog. Coming here was a fool's errand. She'd given her mother false hope when she'd agreed to come back to Texas for the month between finishing her epidemiology certification and waiting for the job in Atlanta…assuming she got the CDC job.

Her only explanation for caving into Momma's invitation had to be the twin extremes of euphoria and exhaustion she'd experienced at the fancy graduation dinner Momma threw in one of New York's finest restaurants.

"You wouldn't believe how your brother's oldest has grown," Momma had said as she smeared butter on a roll and continued her update on life in Mt. Hope. "Jamie's still small for four, but despite his early start, he's as smart as his Aunt Maddie. And little Libby's blonde curls remind me of how much hair you had at three months. They all would've been here for your proud moment, but Amy just wasn't up to traveling after her rough delivery. Thank God for Dr. Boyer and his maternal-fetal skills."

The stoplight cycled through all three colors again without a single car passing through from any direction.

She wanted David's children to adore her the way they adored Momma.

She loved kids. In theory.

In practicality, she knew better than to wish for a miracle.

She was awful with children. They either cried or ran the other way whenever she dared to venture into their little worlds. Momma claimed if Maddie would just calm down, kids wouldn't smell her fear. Maddie believed the problem to be far simpler—some people were suited to be parents. Some were not. She broke out in hives whenever she was faced with the care of a tiny human. If that wasn't proof she'd done the right thing when she gave up the idea of practicing family medicine and sought a career in epidemiology, she didn't know what was. Children weren't allowed to infiltrate infectious disease labs.

So far, her long-distance plan of connecting with David's kids by sending gifts worked for her. Why had she agreed to subject herself to the humiliation of failing in person?

Parker Kemp.

His name was a jab to the heart that didn't make a lick of sense. She'd discarded the starry-eyed humanitarian over four years ago. Left him holding a horseshoe at her mother's wedding reception. She'd returned to the medical residency she'd chosen because of the miles it put between her and several unpleasant things. Like the possibility of becoming a missionary's wife. She knew what a life spent in ministry looked like. She'd watched her mother struggle under the constant scrutiny and the inability to measure up to people's expectations. Long hours, constant demands, and poor financial remuneration had sent her father to an early grave.

She'd made the right choice. Medicine, along with the respect and financial security a professional career offered, was the life for her.

And she'd been fine with the decision…until her last phone conversation with Momma.

"Why does Parker have to leave Guatemala?" She regretted taking the bait the minute she bit. Before she could back out, Momma set the hook.

"His ranch manager trashed his house and nearly burned down his barn. Parker's father took over, and he was doing a pretty good job of keeping up with his own cattle operation and Parker's ranch until he got thrown from a horse and broke his hip. Doctors are saying poor Ryan's going to have a protracted recovery—and all of this right during calving season. Parker has no choice. He has to come home. If he can't hire a new manager to cover the ranch until his father is back on his feet, he'll either have to sell his land, or leave his third-world water project for good."

The idea of Parker facing the loss of his dream made her incredibly sad. He deserved to be happy. More than any man she'd ever met. That's why she'd set him free.

On the two-day drive from the East Coast, she'd prepared for the possibility that, despite this setback, Parker *was* happy. That he'd found the perfect someone.

What she hadn't prepared for was how this rugged and suddenly beautiful landscape reminded her of his scuffed boots, big heart, and endearing smile.

Maddie tapped the wheel. Parker was an old friend who would never want to become her new problem.

A horn blasted behind her. With a start, her chin jerked toward the mirror. The impatient cattle truck driver waved at her to move on.

"Okay. I'm going." Maddie flipped her right signal and turned onto Main Street.

She passed the Koffee Kup. The diner windows were dark. Why was the town's only viable restaurant closed earlier than normal on a summer evening? What would the old ranchers who'd worked until dark do for supper? Next door to the diner was the Mt. Hope Messenger, the newspaper office where Momma had been hired on as an obituary writer after Daddy died. Maddie appreciated how Ivan Tucker had given Momma the opportunity to get back into journalism. Across the street, all the businesses had been boarded up except for Dewey's Hardware and Brewer's Auto. Had Momma mentioned the sagging economy, or had she simply not paid attention whenever Mt. Hope came up in their conversations?

Two blocks past the square, the last of the sun's golden rays bounced off the steeple of Mt. Hope Community Church. Maddie steeled herself and wheeled onto Church Street.

Construction on the church's new family life center was almost complete and the parsonage where she'd grown up had undergone a facelift. Apparently, in replacing dad at Mt. Hope Community Church, her big brother hadn't squandered *his* inheritance on fast cars.

Feeling guilty and a little conspicuous in her plush leather seat, Maddie eased the Porsche into the parsonage drive and rolled to a cautious stop in front of the two-story monstrosity she'd once called home. Every light in the house was on and the place sparkled. Momma had spent years chipping away at the coats of paint that held this house together, but the parsonage had never glowed like it did now. Amazing what new siding, windows, and a beautiful front door could do for an old house.

Maddie stared at the hand-lettered banner flapping between freshly-painted front porch pillars.

Welcome HOME, Dr. Harper!!!

The load she carried just got heavier.

"She's here!" Maxine crowed from the porch steps. The long-legged elder's wife leapt to her feet, ran to the front door, and yelled through the screen. "Leona, put down that grandbaby and come quick."

Maddie's designer heels were sinking in the Texas dust when Momma flew out the door, arms open wide.

"My sweet baby girl!"

Baby girl was going to be a tough image to shed. Maddie silently reminded herself that she was a grown woman who'd earned the right to direct her own life. If she had to, she'd remind her mother of that fact.

Momma shimmered in her strappy summer dress and red heels as she raced down the stairs. Hard to tell whether Momma's healthy, sun-kissed glow came from finally being debt-free or from living at the lake with her new husband and his bass boat.

Momma on water.

The thought was almost as jarring as getting used to seeing her mother holding hands with another man. It wasn't that Maddie didn't like Saul Levy. She did. He'd been good for Momma. Kept her distracted and when Momma was distracted she was far less likely to butt into her life. If she had any hope of maintaining this freedom Momma had granted her, Maddie would need Saul's help to divert Momma's disappointment after she announced her decision. But, as much as she admired her mother's new husband, seeing him standing in her father's place on the parsonage porch was harder than she expected.

Momma threw her arms around Maddie in a protective bear hug. "Come here, sweetheart."

"Hey, Momma," Maddie's gaze shot over her mother's shoulder. Half of the congregation of Mt. Hope Community Church had spilled out of the house and joined Saul on the porch. Momma must have asked them to park their cars on the other side of the church to pull off this ambush.

"Surprise!" Everyone shouted in unison.

The mystery as to why Ruthie's diner had been deserted was solved. The prodigal daughter had come home. Momma had asked the town's best cook to kill the fatted calf while she filled the parsonage with a fleet of probing, small-talk middlemen.

Ruthie Crouch held out a piece of her pie. "Chocolate meringue, Maddie. Your favorite."

Maddie whispered into her mother's ear, "Momma, I thought we agreed I was slipping into town to rest for a few weeks."

Her mother pulled back and offered an innocent smile. "It's just a little welcome home celebration. They're as proud of you as I am." Momma patted her cheek. "I know you're tired. They won't stay long, I promise." She lifted the luggage strap from Maddie's shoulder. "Let me get this for you."

Maddie clenched the strap. "I can manage."

"It's not very heavy." Momma won the tug of war then raised the lightweight bag up and down with a confused scowl. "You didn't bring much."

Maddie shot a rescue-me gaze at the only other human on the planet who understood what it meant to have Momma constantly hovering. "Hey, big bro."

"Hey, little sis." How did David do it? Live in the parsonage. Stand in their father's pulpit Sunday after Sunday. Have Momma constantly in his business, and not go mad.

David, and his little family, navigated the porch steps.

The small, blond-headed boy with huge blue eyes perched high on her brother's shoulders couldn't be Jamie. Momma was right. Her nephew had certainly thrived despite his premature birth. David's wife, Amy cradled baby Libby. Although it was obvious from Amy's sunken cheeks that this last pregnancy had taken a toll on her health, the petite nurse still glowed with peace and contentment.

Before Maddie could say how glad she was to see her brother and make a mess of trying to get to know his children, the Story sisters tromped down the steps and formed a parenthetical statement around David's little family. The old women's sun-spotted hands clasped pickle jars and excited grins pleated their wrinkled faces.

Etta May lightly dragged bent fingers hand across Maddie's cheek. "Hasn't she grown into quite the beauty, Sister?"

Nola Gay nodded. "I told you she'd lose that baby fat."

Etta May's silver brows disappeared under her weed-wacked bangs. "And still smart as a whip according to your Momma."

Embarrassment crept up Maddie's neck. "Y'all haven't changed a bit." Maddie cringed at how quickly her Texas drawl had returned.

Nola Gay raised a jar of pickles in salute. "Leona, your young'uns have done you proud."

"Maddie!" Grandmother came out the front door holding tightly to Cotton, Maddie's favorite church janitor. Roberta Worthington had traded in her stiff salon-tease and her pursed lips for an easy wash-and-go cut and a warm, welcoming smile.

Maybe coming home wouldn't be the torture she'd put off for four years.

"Hey, Grandmother," Maddie waved back, surprised at her genuine pleasure in seeing the woman she'd spent most of her life avoiding. "Cotton, you still driving that old truck?"

"Bessie's runnin' like a top." Everyone knew Cotton could afford a fleet of new pickups after his brilliant investment strategies had made him and the Harpers filthy rich. "Had to put a new clutch in her after you learned how to drive." He nodded toward her Porsche. "I see you still love speed."

Maddie shrugged, remembering her recent interstate loss. "She's responsive, but I bet your Bessie could smoke her on the line."

"Well, that's a bet I'll take you up on," Cotton said.

Maddie scanned the porch again.

No Parker.

Feeling disappointed that he wasn't here to greet her was stupid. She knew better than to expect him, even if he was in town.

Maxine nodded toward Maddie's new car. "How was your cross-country drive?"

"It's not a Cadillac, but it got me here."

"Your momma's been worryin' about you for the past two days." Maxine continued to commandeer the conversation in her typical my-husband-is-chairman-of-the-church-board manner. Or was he? Maddie hadn't asked Momma what happened after that Sunday Maxine melted down and accused Howard of having an affair. From their smiles, either the couple had made their peace, or they were just grateful they'd come to the end of the years of intensive marriage counseling Momma had put them through. The last time Maddie had seen Maxine she was sedated and broken. Seeing her whole and hopeful was a pleasant surprise.

Maddie shifted in her heels. "Nellie in town?"

"She's out at Parker's ranch helping Kathy with the chores while Ryan is laid up," Maxine minus her usual malice was as disconcerting as her heartfelt, "She's anxious to see you."

Nellie doing manual labor was almost as hard to imagine as Nellie being glad to see her.

"We can't figure out what's keeping Parker," Etta May said.

Maddie smoothed the interest from her face. "Was our wandering county extension agent supposed to be here tonight?"

"Should have been here days ago," Nola Gay said. "We took some pickles out to Parker's parents this afternoon. His mother is worried sick." Nola Gay held up her mason jar. "These are the last of the crop Parker saved from those nasty beetles."

Memories of Parker patiently helping two old women protect their cucumber crop flashed in Maddie's head. "Hasn't he called?"

Before Nola Gay could answer, Ivan Tucker squeezed Maddie against her mother. "Would you two mind hugging again?" Ivan raised his camera. "I wanted a candid shot, but I got Leona's backside in the first one, and I know better than to print a wide angle on the front page."

Everyone laughed. Momma blushed and waved Ivan off.

"Hug her again, Leona," Maxine shouted. "Hug your girl."

Aunt Roxie, Momma's best friend and Maddie's only reliable link to the outside world while she was growing up said, "Hell's bells, Ivan. Give them a minute." She raised her long fingers to her ruby lips and blew Maddie a commiserating kiss.

"I'm happy to hold my baby until the cows come home." Momma handed Maddie's suitcase off to David and wrapped her in another breath-robbing embrace.

Laughter bubbled over despite Maddie's concern for Parker's delay. "I wish Daddy could have been here."

Momma squeezed her hard. "He would have been so proud." They'd never really talked about Daddy's heart attack and Momma's summoning wave to David meant they weren't having that honest conversation now. "Y'all, let Aunt Madison see how much my grandbabies have grown."

Maddie's beaming sister-in-law carefully lifted the lightweight blanket from the face of the baby cradled in her arms. "She's asleep," Amy whispered as she held out little Libby.

Maddie's heart raced. Sweat beaded her top lip. Everyone was expecting her to hold the baby. But she wasn't about to embarrass herself by waking the little angel and causing her to scream. Luckily, she'd been trained to think on her feet. She reached into her oversized handbag and pulled out the pink bunny she'd bought at a gas station outside Abilene. Standing as close as she dared, she peered inside the blanket. "She's beautiful."

David bounced his son on his shoulders. "Like her momma." Little Jamie giggled and plunged his fingers into his father's thick hair. The boy pulled back on the strands like he was stopping a horse. David's cringe told her the fierce tugs hurt, but instead of chastising his son, he said, "Jamie, can you tell Aunt Maddie, hello?"

Her nephew eyed her warily, frowned, then shook his head.

"I brought you a surprise too, Jamie." Maddie retrieved a plastic helicopter from her purse. She'd agonized between the chopper and the kid-sized firefighter suit. In the end, she'd gone with the gift that would fit in her car's tiny trunk. Obviously, from Jamie's wrinkled nose, thinking of herself had been the wrong choice. "Look, the light flashes." She pressed the button then held out her last-minute offering.

The curly-headed blond buried his face in his daddy's hair, sending a clear message: he wanted no part of her or her silly gas station toy.

"I'll just let your dad keep it for you, okay?"

"Sorry, sis." David hooked one arm across Jamie's legs to keep him secure and took the helicopter with his free hand. "He takes a while to warm up to folks."

"So do I." Truth be known, she was relieved Jamie hadn't leapt into her arms. With the maternal gene missing from her DNA, who knew what might have happened. "Momma, what's going on with Parker?"

"We don't know. He said he'd be on the next plane." Momma shook her head. "That was days ago."

"Has anyone tried calling him?" Maddie immediately regretted her condescending tone.

"Of course."

"I didn't mean…"

David interrupted, "He's not answering his phone and no one at the mountain clinic will give us any information."

"We don't need to burden your sister." Momma wouldn't win any acting awards. She was clearly irritated that Maddie had come home so prickly.

Frankly, Maddie was irritated at herself. Getting off on the wrong foot was not going to help her win total freedom. "I want to hear, Momma."

"I'm sure he had things to wrap up on his wonderful water project. It's just taking longer than he anticipated." Momma hooked her arm through Maddie's. "There's a plate of fudge inside with your name on it."

Thirty minutes later, Maddie was in the process of turning down Bette Bob's second offering of chocolate fudge and worrying about what could have delayed Parker's return to the States when Shirley's cell phone rang.

The church secretary looked at her caller ID then signaled for quiet. "It's Kathy."

Hush fell over the room. Shirley put a finger in one ear and raised the phone to the other. Maddie couldn't breathe as Shirley's face scrunched into dismay. "Oh no...are you sure...I'll tell them...of course, dear, prayer goes without saying." She clicked off her phone and turned. The color had drained from Shirley's face. "They've found Parker." Checking to make sure she had everyone's attention, she shook her head slowly and added, "It's not good."

Maddie's stomach dropped. "Where is he?"

"Still in Guatemala." Shirley gulped like what she had to say next was stuck in her throat. "They say he's...dying."

Everyone gasped. Maddie suddenly couldn't breathe.

David rushed to Shirley's side and led her to a chair. "Tell us everything Kathy said."

Shirley's head bobbed up and down as she tried to recall the entire conversation. "Someone from that mountain village where Parker's been livin' hauled him to the nearest city in the back of a pickup. They couldn't call Parker's mother until they got him to the hospital." Shirley lifted teary eyes. "They think he has the typhoid."

All heads swiveled toward Maddie.

The facts of this bacterial illness whirled in her head. "The odds are slim if his vaccinations are current." No one moved. "He is current, right, Shirley?"

Finally, Shirley shrugged helplessly. "He's been gone four years."

"A proper course of antibiotics should have him back on his feet in a few days," Maddie couldn't hide her wariness at the probability of his case being handled properly.

Momma's lips trembled. "And if he's not had the care he needed?"

Maddie felt devoured by the roomful of eyes hungry for hope. Improper treatment of Parker's illness could lead to a perforated intestine or even death. "I won't know until I get there, Momma."

CHAPTER TWO

Maddie didn't think she'd ever get used to her mother having the means, or the hospital connections, to charter a medevac plane with one phone call. Wealth had been a lucky turn to her mother's life, but she wasn't about to entrust her life to chance. She wanted to control her own destiny.

The pilot's warning to prepare for arrival echoed in the medically-outfitted cabin.

Maddie snapped her seatbelt and watched out a small window as the plane dropped through the dark clouds building over the active Guatemalan lava dome of Santa María. The narrow streets of Quetzaltenango snaked around the volcano's rugged base. Maddie hadn't seen the crowded mountain city in over a decade. She'd not forgotten how enchanted she'd been by her first glimpse of Central America or how much she'd loved her time here.

The summer between her sophomore and junior year of college, her parents scraped together three thousand dollars so she could spend two months wiping noses at a small clinic perched high in the jungle. Momma had hoped the trip would reignite Maddie's cooling faith. Instead, watching people die because of inadequate health care had done just the opposite. How could a loving God take a mother from her children or a child from its mother? If she'd been a doctor, she could have made a real difference.

It was in these mountains that she'd made the decision to return to college, change her major from family counseling to bio-chemistry, and to put her faith behind her. By the time her father died, her faith was beyond resurrection.

Now this lush land threatened to change her life again.

If anything happened to Parker, who could she count on? Not that she'd called on him during the rough ride of her medical residency. But in the back of her mind, she'd always known she could.

Until now.

She'd managed to gather a few more facts from Parker's mother as she'd waited for the charter to arrive at Mt. Hope's small municipal airport. Parker had become ill the same day he was scheduled to begin his journey back to Texas. During a quick call, he'd complained of a bad stomachache, but he'd assured his mother it was probably something he ate. He couldn't be far from the outhouse, but the moment he thought he could make the bus ride to the airport, he would. It had been five days since she'd heard his beautiful voice. He'd quit answering her calls or texts.

Kathy went on to say that Parker had spent the past few weeks working to clear up a sewage leak which was suspected to be the cause of the typhoid outbreak in the village. When Parker checked in at the poorly staffed and overrun mountain clinic, they'd assured him that vaccinated Americans didn't get typhoid. So they'd treated him with Acetaminophen and sent him back to his rented room to ride it out.

Maddie didn't have the heart to tell Kathy that her assurances about Parker's vaccinations had been for the benefit of everyone at Momma's party. Truth was the typhoid vaccine had an effectiveness-rating of less than seventy percent. Arbitrarily deciding Parker had not contracted typhoid was a mistake. Early diagnosis and proper treatment was essential for recovery. She wouldn't know Parker's prognosis until she was able to examine him, run some tests, and talk to his caregivers.

Her attempts to contact Gabriella had been unsuccessful. The beautiful South Texas College nursing student who'd interned with Maddie had found the Lord in these mountains. They'd kept in touch at first…long enough for Maddie to know Gabriella had returned to the small village clinic after her graduation. Maddie could only hope it had been Gabriella who'd attended Parker. Gabriella would have sent him to a medical facility in the city for proper testing and treatment.

The plane skimmed treetops bent under a sudden deluge of rain then slid to a stop just short of a row of trees. Maddie gathered her backpack filled with her stethoscope and a couple of rounds of antibiotics to tide Parker over during his extraction and return home. The pilot climbed out of his seat and opened the jet door.

Rain pounded the tarmac. Despite the midday heat, a cold ache crept into Maddie's core. Sloshing around in a jungle sauna to rescue a man who hadn't bothered to write in four years was a man who apparently had no interest in reviving their old friendship.

She raised her backpack over her head and raced into the canary-yellow cinder block terminal. Spanish stormed her ears. Lucky for her, working New York's emergency rooms had kept her fluency skills sharp. The addition of modern cash machines in the airport terminal gave her hope that Parker had been sent to an updated hospital and was receiving proper medical care.

Soaked to the skin and breathing hard from the higher altitude, Maddie searched the terminal's limited signage. The tempting aroma of spicy food stirred her empty stomach. With the possibility of typhoid in the region, she wasn't willing to consume street vendor tamales wrapped in banana leaves that could have been washed in tainted water. She turned away from the portable food court and hurried toward the smell of diesel and the swirl of black smoke. The Story twins had reissued their usual warning to stay clear of the chicken buses. According to Maddie's Google search, a bus was safer than a taxi and since the hospital was clear across town, she didn't have time to walk. Surely, a country sporting modern ATM machines had improved its transportation system as well, she told herself.

And then, she saw the bus. The dilapidated eight-passenger van belched sooty fumes.

Holding her bag to her chest, Maddie poked her head through the vehicle's sliding door. Scents of unwashed bodies, animals, and poverty brought one hand to her nose. She asked a woman to pass her phone to the driver so he could see the text from Parker's mother with the hospital name and address. The driver passed the phone back and nodded toward the rear of the van. A woman holding a chicken, and a man who hadn't shaved in several days, scooted apart and waved her toward the sliver of space.

"Why do I never listen?" Maddie mumbled in English as she climbed over the legs of a skinny boy.

When she'd Googled the city's local hospitals, she was surprised to learn a private hospital had been built in Quetzaltenango since her last visit. She really hoped Parker had been taken to this new facility. It wasn't much to brag about, but at least it had a couple of five-star ratings and the grainy website video touted modern equipment.

As the van chugged down a street lined with restored neoclassical architecture dating back to the 19th-century, coffee-boom days, Maddie remained hopeful. Then the van turned a corner. The streets quickly gave way to shanties constructed from tin and cardboard. Parker had been taken to the public hospital…a facility with no stars and multiple warnings against going there unless you were bleeding to death.

Maddie snugged the backpack against her roiling stomach. The chicken studied her with beady eyes. If it had been anyone else but Parker stranded down here, she'd be pecking her way out of this deathtrap.

What had happened to that girl who came home from the jungle intent on saving the world? The thought was a guilty slap to her conscience.

She had the training. She had the money. But now, she didn't have the guts. Parker had done what she'd only talked about. If he wasn't dead by the time she got to him, she'd kill him for making her face the jungle, poor medical conditions, and so much poverty the entire Harper fortune couldn't make a dent. The futility of the situation in the heart of Central America had broken her heart then. The lack of progress sickened her now.

The bus puttered to a stop in front of a peeling-paint bungalow with bars on the windows.

"*El hospital.*" The driver shouted over his shoulder.

Maddie leaned around the chicken and stared at the desolate structure. "This can't be it."

The driver pointed to his empty palm.

Maddie paid the fare and climbed out. The rain had slowed to a drizzle, but her frizzy curls were beyond saving. Not bothering to raise her backpack, she made her way through the gnarled trees. She pushed open the wooden door. Smells reminiscent of the nursing home her parents used to make her visit once a month hung heavy in the sweltering air. She waited for her eyes to adjust to the dim lighting. A woman dressed in the American equivalent of scrubs was hurrying toward her.

"Are you bleeding?" she asked hopefully in Spanish.

Maddie shook her head, dusted off her fluent Spanish, and responded, "I'm looking for a friend." She pulled out her phone. "Americano." She presented the woman with her screensaver photo, a picture of her laughing with a tall, handsome man throwing a horseshoe at Momma's wedding. Aunt Roxie had captured the beautiful moment of them enjoying each other's company for the last time. She'd texted it as a consolation prize after Maddie finally found the courage to set Parker free. "A patient. Parker Kemp." The woman's wary scowl pushed Maddie into Code Blue mode. "I'm his American doctor, and I want to see him. NOW."

From the woman's nod, Maddie knew the woman had understood every word of her request. When she spun in the direction of the five rooms in this tiny place, Maddie hurriedly followed after her.

The yeasty smell of typhoid hit Maddie's nose the moment the door to Parker's room opened.

"Oh, no." She rushed to the small metal bed filled with a man's limp 6'4" frame. "Parker?" She leaned in. Beneath the sour odor of sickness, she detected the faint scent of Aqua Velva. He'd worn this cologne since the day he showed up in Sunday school with little pieces of bloody toilet paper stuck to his chin. A sweaty curl clung to the scar on his forehead, the scar he'd gotten the night he came to save her. She brushed away the wet strand. He felt too warm for someone who'd been dosed with proper antibiotics. "Let me see his chart," Maddie barked in Spanish.

"Lucia," the woman said in perfect English. "My name is Lucia." And from her crossed arms, Lucia did not appreciate an American doctor bursting in on her patient and telling her what to do.

"Lucia, I'm concerned by his toxic appearance." Maddie stomped around the bed and helped herself to his chart. "He's been here nearly…seventy-two hours. Seventy-two hours and he still has a fever?" She stared at the single page. "Chloramphenicol? No one uses that anymore."

"Maddie?" The sound of Parker's gravelly voice made her heart skip a beat.

She whipped around. Parker was struggling to open his eyes. She closed the chart, leaned close, and whispered. "Parker."

"You smell like a wet dog."

"And you smell like a dinner roll." Maddie straightened and pushed a strand of wet hair behind her ears. "Do you know what that tells me?"

"It's Thanksgiving?"

"It tells me you probably have typhoid. I thought I told you not to make me come down here to save your sorry butt and—"

His heavy eyelids were barely cooperating, forcing him to scrunch to focus. "And yet, here you are."

Unwilling to let herself get lost in his continued belief in her selflessness, she spouted, "Somebody has to keep you from killing yourself."

"Don't make a fuss." His weak smile stopped the lecture forming on her tongue. Maybe he was in better shape than she thought. His crooked index finger motioned her closer. "Tell Isabella she's pretty." His eyes drifted closed. "And that I love her."

"Isabella?" Maddie took a step back. "Who's Isabella?"

He didn't answer. Was he delusional? Or had he found someone and moved on? The possibility was a sledgehammer to her chest.

"He's been talking out of his head since he arrived," the woman in scrubs explained in very good English. "The antibiotics don't seem to be working."

"Because you have him on the wrong one."

"We have nothing else."

"No Cipro?"

"No."

Maddie ripped Parker's gown up. Her gaze bolted past his lack of underwear. Rose spots covered his lower chest and distended abdomen. She pressed one of the spots. The welt blanched under pressure, but Parker remained unresponsive to her touch. "How long has he been on the Chloramphenicol?"

The nurse looked at her watch. "Forty-eight hours."

Possible complications from a drug-resistant Salmonella typhi spooled in Maddie's head. She didn't have enough Cipro to risk letting him ride this out here. If his bowel perforated, she'd have between six to twelve hours before he became septic. Moving him across town didn't guarantee access to a full drug regimen, or the highly-skilled surgeons he'd need to give him a fighting chance. She could fly him home in less than three hours. "I need an ambulance STAT."

"Why?"

"Because he'll die if he stays here."

Maddie was used to people responding to her orders, but American doctors had no clout here. This nurse took her time finding the doctor to sign Parker's release. The ambulance had a flat tire on its way to the hospital. No one could tell her when the tire would be fixed. And Parker kept asking for Isabella. To keep from climbing out of her skin, Maddie monitored Parker's vitals in-between checking her watch and pacing.

Frustrated at the lack of progress toward securing Parker's release, Maddie snatched a fresh trash liner from an empty bin. She stormed to the chair by Parker's bed loaded with a pile of his personal belongings. "I'm going to get you out of this dump before they kill you," she whispered as she dropped his underwear in the bag. "Leave everything to me." Next, she stuffed Parker's scuffed cowboy boots into the trash bag. The heels were worn and there was a dime-sized hole in one of the soles. She tossed his threadbare flannel shirt in with the boots. His jeans were shredded at the knees, not because Parker had paid attention to the latest fashion trend, but because he'd had these Levi's since high school. She knew this because the back pocket still had the swipe of yellow paint she'd dragged across his backside during their last youth group service project. That was nearly thirteen years ago. Refusing to believe he'd kept the jeans as a reminder of their high school flirtation, she wadded the pants. His phone fell out of the front pocket and bounced on the Saltillo tile.

Praying the screen hadn't cracked, she grabbed the phone. The case, sleek, silver and obviously new, was such a contrast to his other possessions. She turned the phone over. A picture of a silky-haired brunette wearing pale blue scrubs and a stunning smile flashed onto the screen.

Gabriella?

Before Maddie could make a positive ID, the screen reverted to black. Maddie's thumb hovered over the home button. If the beautiful nurse from the mountain clinic was Parker's screensaver choice, why did he keep calling for someone named Isabella?

Maddie glanced at Parker moving fitfully in his sleep. He seemed as confused as she was. For all she knew, he'd mixed-up Gabriella's name with the people he rented a room from or perhaps he'd taken in a stray dog while living here.

But what if she'd misunderstood him? What if he was really saying *Gabriella* instead of *Isabella*? After all, he was dehydrated, and his throat was very dry.

Searching for clues, Maddie tilted the phone again. The woman in the photo was definitely Gabriella. No question about it. Were Gabriella and Parker a couple? Possible. But if that was the case, then where was Gabriella? Maddie had lost touch with the girl she'd bunked with for one entire summer, but she remembered the beautiful nurse as a loyal and dedicated friend. If Gabriella had, in any way, returned Parker's infatuation, she'd be at his side right now.

Maddie moved her thumb away from the phone's home button. Satisfying her curiosity didn't give her the right to invade Parker's privacy. Once she had him tethered to proper antibiotics, he'd be up and around in no time. Then he could call whomever he wanted…Gabriella…Isabella…as long as he was no longer fraternizing with Salmonella, she couldn't care less whom he hung out with.

As she slipped his phone into the bag with his clothes, Lucia brought the doctor into the room and announced, "The ambulance is here."

"Finally." Maddie growled as she signed off on the transfer of care. She should be calm now, her worry banished because she'd have Parker settled into a decent medical facility in a few hours. She'd been raised to be sweet, but ever since her father died it didn't take much to stir up her anger. "You better hope I get him home before his bowels perforate and he turns septic." She shoved the gurney toward the door and nearly plowed into a woman stepping across the threshold. "I'm sorry." Maddie flew around the gurney and examined the legs of the little girl the woman was holding. "Are either of you hurt?"

The woman shook her head and checked the toddler. "We're good."

"Great." Maddie shot back around the gurney. "I'm in a hurry. Could you move please?" Incensed that the woman who'd clearly entered the wrong room just stood there staring at her, Maddie snapped, "This is an emergency."

"Where are you taking our Parker?" the woman asked in Spanish.

Maddie's grip tightened on the bed railing. "You know him?"

The woman's eyes widened as she took in Parker's condition. "He's the big farmer who fixes our well. He rents a bed and a baby crib from me."

"A crib?"

"For his daughter," the woman cut her eyes toward the dark-eyed girl in her arms. "She's been crying for her father."

Maddie shook her head. "There's been some mistake."

"No mistake, senorita."

"I would know if Parker had a child."

The woman bristled at Maddie's accusation. "I no lie."

Parker coughed then grimaced as if every muscle in his body ached.

Maddie took a deep breath. "This man doesn't have time for wells or children." She pressed her lips. Yelling at everyone was not going to get Parker on that plane. "I'm sure someone here can help you sort this out. We need to go."

"The farmer told me a horse had hurt his father. That is why he was packing to take his daughter to America. Then the diarrhea came. The clinic said my tamales had made him sick. When he got worse, I found a man to drive him to the city. I finished packing his daughter, then waited in the rain for the bus." She held out a soggy bag woven from brightly-colored grasses. "The farmer is a good man."

As the woman who smelled of cooking fires and damp hemp squeezed past the gurney, the little girl lunged for Parker. "Paki."

Parker's heavy eyelids fluttered open. "Isabella?" He raised his hands a couple of inches off the bed. "Come to Daddy."

CHAPTER THREE

S torm clouds, dark as the confusion swirling in Maddie's head, gathered over the mountains as she watched the ambulance attendants pull Parker's gurney from the ambulance.

Typhoid tended to cluster in families. Had Parker contracted the illness from water contaminated by his own daughter's dirty diapers?

His daughter?

The child had called him *paki*. Was that a toddler version of *papi*, the Spanish name for father? Or was *paki* some sort of nickname? Like a name given to a favorite uncle or dear friend. She really wished she'd taken Momma up on her offer to accompany her on this trip. All those years of teaching the two-year-old Sunday school class had made Momma a master at interpreting childish gibberish.

Hurt throbbed in Maddie's chest as she studied the little girl who'd finally fallen asleep on a reclined plane seat. Maddie had been rendered immobile when Parker's insistent landlady shoved the toddler into her arms before she could board the charter.

"She's eighteen months old and terrified," the woman had stated like Maddie should know.

"But I can't take her."

The woman had pointed to Parker's gurney being lifted into the medevac plane. "If he's your friend, you will take her for him."

She wheeled, and left Maddie the bag, or at least that's how this squirming child had felt in her arms. Parker was her friend, no matter how much it stung that he'd kept something this life-changing from her.

The pilot stepped to the open jet door. "If we're going to beat this weather, we need to go."

She may not know much about children, but she would never abandon a child, especially one Parker obviously loved.

Maddie checked Parker's IV and his vitals. She'd done all she could do until they were home. She let her gaze drift to the mystery child. Why had she allowed herself to be pushed around? For all she knew, this woman had seen an opportunity to send her own child abroad for medical care. Maddie stepped forward and lightly touched the girl's tiny forehead. The child stirred. Maddie jerked her hand back. Other than being exhausted from a night of traveling, the toddler didn't feel warm to the touch. She may appear to be perfectly healthy, but she'd still have to be tested for typhoid when they reached Mt. Hope. Simultaneously running a DNA test on the kid crossed Maddie's mind as well.

Which was pure craziness. And none of her business.

But none of what had happened since her arrival in a country she still secretly loved made any sense...unless...Parker had gotten married. The possibility was another kick in the gut she found hard to believe. Parker would have told his mother and his mother would have told Momma and Momma wouldn't have been able to keep a disappointment of that scale to herself.

The only other scenario was almost as crazy as the idea of her risking her medical license to run a secret DNA test. Parker might not have married Isabella's mother. After all, he'd been gone a long time. People get lonely. Lines get blurred. She'd fallen victim to both of those traps. But wrapping her mind around the possibility that Parker had randomly slept with someone and fathered a child was impossible. Parker believed in old-fashioned relationships: love, marriage, and then baby carriages. He wouldn't keep his parents in the dark about a woman who'd given him a child he obviously adored.

The man on the gurney was too delirious to interrogate now. That's why she'd made the decision to text Momma before the medevac charter took off for Texas. Not details. Only that she and Parker were en route and that when they landed, they would need an ambulance...and a car seat.

Except for the addition of a baby, this skewed rescue trip was reminiscent of the time Parker drove all the way to Dallas in a blizzard to pick her up at the airport. On the way back to Mt. Hope, they'd spun out in the snow and totaled Parker's truck. Parker had suffered a head injury. Maddie had been so terrified of losing him, she'd kissed him.

Hard.

For the past four years, she'd thought about that kiss off and on. Sometimes, she'd even wondered what it would have been like if she'd chosen to go with him and kiss him every day for the rest of her life. But right now, all she wanted to do was smack him.

Hard.

Maddie rummaged through her backpack and retrieved the flimsy paper Isabella's caregiver had also shoved into her hands. The legal document was written in Spanish and stamped with an official-looking seal.

Maddie could decipher scattered phrases, but she had no trouble recognizing Parker's sloppy signature. The man had agreed to something, and from the looks of it, he was now legally bound.

"It is proof of Parker's right to take the child from the country," Lucia had said when Maddie asked for a quick translation.

Maddie folded the paper and slid it into the trash bag with Parker's belongings. She unfastened her seatbelt and assessed Parker's condition for the tenth time. Fever was still high, but his lack of intense abdominal pain gave her hope that with proper treatment he could avoid developing a leak in his intestines.

She checked her watch. According to the pilot, they'd touch down in Mt. Hope in less than thirty minutes. Momma's curiosity about the need for a car seat couldn't possibly rival Maddie's growing need for answers. She reached inside the trash bag and pulled out Parker's phone. A slight tilt of the device brought up the screensaver again. She gasped. She'd been so focused on trying to figure out why Gabriella's photo was Parker's favorite pic that she'd missed the dark-haired baby on the nurse's hip.

Isabella.

Maddie glanced from the sleeping child back to the child on the screen. It was her. A few months younger, but the dark-haired beauty in Gabriella's arms was the same child Parker's landlady had insisted he would never leave.

Had Parker fallen in love with Gabriella? Was the nurse Maddie had admired and trusted the mother of Parker's child? Maddie shoved the pieces of this puzzle around in her brain like shards of a shattered mirror.

Gabriella was everything Maddie was not. Kind. Compassionate. Gentle. A lover of children. Maddie dropped the phone back in the trash bag. She was letting emotions get the best of her. Jumping to unfounded conclusions. Isabella most likely had been a motherless child brought to the clinic for care. If so, then how did Isabella's care get sloughed off on Parker?

Nerve endings sparking with unanswered questions, Maddie yanked open a small overhead bin. She removed a blanket and carefully draped the sleeping child.

"I wish you could talk, little one," Maddie whispered as she sunk into the seat opposite the little girl.

She studied Isabella's features for parentage clues that might definitively exclude Parker. She dismissed their matching hair, eyes, and skin tone. Most of Latin America's population had Parker's darker coloring. It was the unique similarities that made a strong paternity case against him.

Wispy, dark curls had escaped the child's high-placed pigtails and stuck to her skin…exactly like Parker's curls clung to his face when he became overheated. The child's long legs were folded close to her chest the same way Parker used to curl his lanky frame into a bus seat on their high school mission trips. Lengthy, thick lashes—exact replicas of the fringe on Parker's lids—rested on her chubby cheeks. No doubt about it, Parker Kemp was written all over this enchanting little thing.

Maddie leaned forward for a closer look. Isabella's eyelids flew open. Two midnight-black eyes studied her back. Afraid to make any sudden moves, the only thing Maddie could think to do was to simply return the child's stare. To her surprise, Isabella's eyes didn't immediately tear up.

"Paki?" the little girl asked without moving.

"He's sleeping." Maddie pointed to the gurney strapped into place. "Right there."

Isabella's tiny face puckered. "Paki?" She slowly sat up and stretched her neck for a better look at Parker. "Paki?" Her lip began to quiver.

Unwilling to spend the rest of the flight with an inconsolable child, Maddie searched the cabin for a distraction. She remembered the granola bar in her backpack. "Are you hungry?" Once again, she was met with a trusting stare. Maddie opened the snack bar. Before she held it out, she did her best to ascertain if the kid had teeth. It was Parker she wanted to choke, not the child. "*¿Tienes hambre?*" she asked in Spanish. Relieved by Isabella's toothy smile, she broke off a small piece of the crumbly oatmeal.

Isabella's mouth opened like a little bird.

Maddie chuckled and offered the pieces in her palm. Isabella took it cautiously from her and ate the bite quickly, then held out her empty hand.

Surprised the child hadn't reacted like her nephew and run screaming to the other end of the plane, Maddie asked, "More?"

Isabella's lips immediately stretched into a big smile. "Peeze," she said in very good English.

"You little stinker. You could understand me all along." Feeling as if she was trying to lure a wild creature close, Maddie smiled and offered Isabella another piece. "You wouldn't want to explain all of this to me, would you?"

Isabella chomped granola happily.

"Didn't think so." She handed Isabella another small piece. "Well, my name is Maddie. Can you say, Maddie?"

"Maa-d." Isabella's attempt sounded like a cross between a calf crying for its mother and mad.

Maddie gave her another piece. "Close enough."

When the last crumb was gone, Isabella folded both hands in her lap like an old lady, cocked her head, and looked at Maddie expectantly. Her big doe eyes seemed to say: *Now what?*

Now what, indeed?

Parker wasn't physically able to run interference for her, and that little snack diversion had taken all of two minutes. They had at least another twenty-five minutes before she could pass Isabella into the capable hands of Momma. Maddie scanned the cabin for another distraction. Tubes and monitors didn't seem like age-appropriate entertainment.

"Want to look out the window?" Maddie motioned to the seatbelt cinching Isabella's waist. "I can let you out until the pilot says we're ready to land." She undid the clasp and Isabella sprung across the aisle and into Maddie's arms. The agile little girl wrapped herself around Maddie's neck and waist tight as a little capuchin monkey. "I can't breathe." Maddie peeled Isabella's arms free, but the kid just flung them around her neck again. "Okay, then." Being squeezed tight by a child sent a warm flush pulsing through Maddie's veins. Was it fear? A sudden realization that her biological clock was ticking? Or was it the terrifying possibility that she was actually enjoying this?

Toting Isabella, Maddie scooted to a seat close to the window and tried to banish the sensation by distracting herself as well. "See the clouds?"

Isabella craned her neck until her nose touched the glass. "Cowds," she repeated.

Maddie couldn't help but chuckle at Isabella's pronunciation of words minus Ls. Just to hear the child's interesting speech pattern again, she asked, "What's your name?"

"Isbaya."

"Ah. That's a smart name for a smart little girl." The jet hit a pocket of turbulence and Maddie and Isabella reached for each other simultaneously. "Whoa." Maddie looked down and Isabella was looking up at her with a trusting intensity. "We better buckle you in again."

"No." Isabella threw her arms around Maddie's neck and pulled her tight.

"But you could get hurt."

"No."

Well, she was certainly as stubborn as Parker that was for sure. "Okay, then. We'll strap in together." Maddie reached behind her, retrieved the seatbelt then snapped herself and Isabella into place. She chanced a downward glance at the little body pressed against her chest. Once again, the little face was pointed up at hers. This time the expression on Isabella's face was total contentment.

Before she could stop herself, Maddie unstuck the curl from Isabella's cheek. "We'll be home soon, little one."

"Home." Isabella plastered the side of her face against the pounding in Maddie's chest.

Questions of why Parker had a child and had kept it a secret were still scrambling Maddie's brain when the jet's wheels smoked the Mt. Hope Municipal Airport runway.

Getting answers would have to wait. The flashing lights of Charlie Copeland's ambulance raced to meet the plane. No one in Mt. Hope wanted Parker to die. Especially, not her.

Because once he was well, she intended to kill him.

CHAPTER FOUR

A hot, dusty smell reminiscent of a West Texas wind roused Parker from the deep sleep that held him captive.

Home.

He willed his heavy eyelids to open. The curly blonde he'd had a crush on his whole life was stroking his face.

Home, and Maddie?

He had to be dreaming. Surely the familiar voice barking orders on his behalf didn't belong to the girl who'd made it clear their lives were headed in opposite directions.

"Mad—?" Her name stuck in his dry throat the way thoughts of kissing her had stuck in his thick skull for far too long.

Someone patted his shoulder. "Parker, it's your mother."

He turned his head away from the vision of Maddie. "Mom?"

"Kathy, we need to get them both to the hospital." He heard that impatient voice directed at him since their shared middle-school days.

"Mads—?" he tried to say again, but her name couldn't get past the sour taste in his mouth.

"Is the baby sick, too?" Why was his mother asking Maddie about a baby?

Maddie shrugged. "She's not exhibiting any signs, but she'll need to be tested."

That's when he noticed the child with chubby arms wrapped around Maddie's neck. Not just any child. His child. He tried to sit up, but none of his limbs would cooperate.

Maddie peeled the child free and held her out to Parker's mother. "All's she had to eat since we took off was a granola bar."

"You gave this poor baby granola?" His mother's uncharacteristically curt response should have been directed at him. He was the one who hadn't told her about his daughter. "Does she even have teeth?"

"It's all I had," Maddie shouted over the mounting cries of Isabella insisting she be returned to Maddie. "And yes, she has teeth."

"I don't think she likes me." His mother juggled his crying daughter on her hip, tears forming behind her glasses. "What if she never likes me?"

"We'll think of something to settle her down." Leona Harper wrapped an assuring arm around his mom. If his old pastor's wife was in his dream, he must be dying, which would explain the terrible pain in his belly. "I've borrowed a car seat from David," Leona went on to say. "Kathy, I'll take the baby in my car and you can follow us to the hospital in the truck."

"A grandchild?" His mother sniffed. "How could he—"

Parker tried to lift his hand, but he was weak as a tomato seedling and feeling just as green.

"What's her name?" Kathy asked.

"Isabella." Maddie stepped between him and his mother. "Kathy, I know this is all a shock, but Parker requires immediate medical attention. We need to go."

His mother's free hand grabbed hold of the gurney. "Maybe your momma can stay with Isabella, and I can take care of my boy."

"Parker's going to the ER, and then into isolation," Maddie explained. "He won't be seeing anybody but me." While Maddie looked at her mother, he searched his old flame's left hand. No ring. His Adam's apple did that thing it used to do whenever she came around…grew way too big for his throat and completely shut off his ability to form words.

Maddie, on the other hand, remained in complete control of her faculties. "Momma, can you escort Isabella and Kathy to the ER?"

"Whatever they need," Leona said. "And I've asked Saul to take over the job of getting your temporary privileges at the hospital sorted out. It may take a few days . . . until then you'll have to work with Dr. Boyer."

"The maternal-fetal specialist you hired for Amy?" Maddie sounded equally confused and miffed.

"Dr. Boyer is our newly appointed chief of staff."

"Long as she stays out of my way, we'll be fine."

"She's a he," Leona corrected. "And he's proven himself quite capable."

"How did he manage to become chief so fast?"

"It's a long story."

"Then you'll have to explain later, Momma." Maddie checked the strap across his chest then gave the ambulance driver the thumbs up. "Charlie, I hope this heap still runs better than it looks."

Charlie wrenched the ambulance door open. "Maybe it ain't fancy as those rigs in the big city, but I ain't lost a patient yet…well, 'cept for your daddy, but he was already in glory by the time I got to the church."

Maddie swallowed hard, as though the guilt of not being around when her father needed her most was the size of a horse-pill. "If you don't get a move on, this poor fellow could be knocking on the pearly gates."

"You always was a bossy little thing." Charlie shoved Parker's gurney into the back of the ambulance.

"Still am." Maddie climbed up and squeezed in beside him. "Call ahead and tell the ER to prepare for an infectious disease arrival."

"Your momma's done warned everyone. She's a one-woman wonder." Charlie locked the gurney in place, glancing over his shoulder to make sure he hadn't been overheard. "Now that Leona's keeping Mt. Hope Memorial afloat, everybody hops to it whenever she speaks." He smiled proudly and slammed the door.

The next time Parker roused, Maddie was standing beside his bed. Her hair was pulled into a messy bun and her clothes were rumpled like she'd been sleeping in them for days. To his gritty eyes, she'd never looked better. He wanted to tell her everything he should have said before he let her walk out of his life, but she was arguing with a tall guy in a white coat and, besides, his Adam's apple was doing that thing again.

"You're a maternal-fetal specialist," Maddie snapped, obviously perturbed she wasn't getting her way. "How many typhoid cases have you treated?"

"I'm just saying, *Dr.* Harper, if you felt this man's condition warranted the supervision of an infectious disease specialist, then why didn't you take him to Dallas?"

"I brought him here, *Dr.* Boyer, because Mt. Hope is his home."

"So, you assessed his condition, without benefit of proper testing, and decided to bring a highly contagious disease into *my* hospital?"

"First of all, since when does being appointed chief make Mt. Hope Memorial *your* hospital? And, secondly, when I assessed the risks against the benefits, I decided Mr. Kemp's *child* had needs as great as his."

"Does she have typhoid?"

"Negative." Maddie squared her shoulders and Parker wanted to shout at the guy with Chris Hemsworth's good looks to take cover, 'cause the girl he'd known most of his life was fixin' to blow. "I know Parker Kemp," Maddie continued. "You don't. And if he, for any reason, felt that his child was in danger or not being cared for properly, the emotional strain would have hindered his recovery."

"Maddie?" Parker croaked.

Her head whipped around. "Hey, stranger." A pleased smile lit her face. "You've had me worried for a couple of days." She reached around the IV tubing and took Parker's hand.

"Dr. Harper, we haven't—"

"Formalities will have to wait, Dr. Boyer. *My* patient is awake."

"Maddie?" Parker whispered.

"Yes?" She leaned over him, her eyes shining with the same tears of relief he'd seen the night he'd plowed them into a snow drift. "It's me, Parker. Can you hear me?"

He waved her closer. The brush of her hair on his cheek awakened desires he'd moved to Guatemala to escape. "Give the poor guy a break."

She pulled back, her brow furrowed. "What?"

"Mr. Kemp," a male voice interrupted. "I'm Robin Boyer, chief of staff here at—"

"*Your* hospital. I heard." Urges, long buried, steamrolled the good sense he'd hoped to acquire in service to others. His gaze darted from the beautiful blonde whose bloodshot blue eyes still danced with the intensity of a range fire to the guy with the chiseled good looks. Barbie and Ken. Matched in looks, smarts, and profession. Much as they probably deserved whatever the other could dish out, he couldn't lay here and let some Madison-Avenue-looking guy take pot shots at his...what? The last time he'd read more into his relationship with Maddie the mistake had pushed her away. He wasn't going to make that mistake again. He quickly settled on *old friend,* then did his best to rally his parched tongue to speak on her behalf. "Maddie wouldn't have come for me if I hadn't been knockin' on the pearly gates. I reckon the thanks for saving my life go to this little lady."

"*Lady* is a generous term," the chief said bluntly.

"You're right," Parker agreed. "Doctor suits her better. Always has." It would be easier to put wind in a bottle than to try and make Maddie into something she was never meant to be. He knew. He'd tried. "I've got typhoid. Don't I, *Dr.* Harper?"

"Yes," she concurred, her expression more miffed than pleased by his defense. "But I was able to get you started on the right meds before your bowels perforated."

"I'll grant that her family medicine and epidemiology credentials are impressive." Dr. Boyer's tight-lipped smile indicated this battle wasn't over. If he was as smart as his title implied, he'd retreat and regroup.

"How long before I can get back in the field?" Parker asked Maddie.

Dr. Boyer took a cautious step toward the bed. "We'll have you out of here as soon as—"

Parker interrupted, "I was asking *my* doctor."

A frustrated sigh huffed between his perfect teeth. "Dr. Harper, once you've explained Mr. Kemp's course of treatment, I'll be waiting in my office to finish our . . . conversation." If it hadn't been for the muscle flinching in the man's clenched jaw, the chief might have sounded almost neighborly.

"Wash your hands before you leave the room, Dr. Boyer," Maddie ordered smugly.

By the time Dr. Boyer had degloved and scrubbed to Maddie's satisfaction, Parker thought he detected smoke coming from the angry doctor's ears.

Maddie waited until the door slammed shut, then she turned what was left of her unspent wrath on Parker. "You've got a lot of explaining to do, mister."

"Good to see you, too." Parker raised his finger, head still throbbing but pleased a little strength was returning to his limbs. "All that savin' *your* butt has made me thirsty."

"Let's be clear on who's saving whom here." She filled the plastic hospital cup and bent the straw. "I'm going to have to adjust the bed." After he was raised, she sat beside him and slid one hand behind his neck. Her hair brushed his cheek again as she lifted the straw to his cracked lips. "How in the world did you contract typhoid?"

Cool liquid snaked down his parched throat. "I'm guessin' the same way anyone does...ingesting tainted water."

"Healthy people who keep their vaccinations current don't usually end up on medevac planes."

He didn't like confessing he'd been foolish, but if confronted with the same choice, he'd gladly make it again. "I let them give my shot to a kid."

"What kid?"

"The one you've been defending."

She swallowed hard and removed her hand from behind his neck. "And how did you get this...kid?"

"Do you mean did I get her the usual way people get kids?" It had been awhile since he'd let himself think about what it would be like to hold Maddie in his arms, but now those images gushed from the well he thought he'd capped. "Or are you asking if I picked her up at the market along with a couple of street tacos?"

"This isn't funny, Parker. Your mom's wiggin' out."

It was as if the mention of his mother and the realization of all he'd left undone suddenly and completely snapped him out of a deep fog. "You didn't have a right to tell my mother anything."

"She knew the girl wasn't mine the minute I stepped off that plane."

"I've got to go." He struggled to try to get out of bed. "Isabella must be scared half to death."

"Calm down, cowboy." Maddie eased him back onto his pillow. "I've heard she's settling in and seems to have finally taken to your mother."

He shook his head. "I promised her she'd never be left alone again." His breath was coming in short little spurts. The gruesome memory of what he'd found buried beneath that mudslide was threatening to bury him. "You've got to bring her to me, Maddie."

Maddie covered him with the sheet. "I'm sorry, but you don't see anybody but me until you've been on the correct antibiotics for a few more days."

CHAPTER FIVE

"You're angry that I cut you off." Dr. Boyer sat behind his desk wearing the same condescending glare he'd used on her in the ER. It hadn't stopped Maddie from taking over the management of the ER's infectious disease protocol, and his smug expression wouldn't stop her from continuing to monitor Parker's care. "That's why you won't consider my offer."

Maddie picked up her backpack. "I don't know what you're talking about, and I really don't care. No way am I giving you a month of family medicine practice in exchange for hospital privileges here." She started for the door.

"A few days ago. Out on I-20. When you gave up at the last minute."

She stopped and turned slowly. "You're the guy in that nasty black convertible."

"You're the girl in the poor-performing Porsche." The same cocky grin he'd flashed that day took over his tanned face. "I'm the guy who beat you then, but I suspect I'll have a fight on my hands if I'm going to beat you now."

This dead-end conversation had circled the obvious resolution long enough. Maddie hadn't slept for more than thirty minutes in nearly three days. She needed a shower and a change of clothes worse than she needed a decent meal. The Cipro she'd prescribed for Parker was working. He was finally out of the woods, and she felt comfortable leaving him for a few hours with the nurse she'd briefed on contagious disease protocol.

"Look, all I need is temporary hospital privileges, only long enough to manage my patient's care for the length of his stay. I'm not asking to take your job, although I'm pretty sure I could get it if I wanted the headache—"

"I admire your mother." The statement stopped her cold. "What she's done for this place has changed healthcare for everyone in this county. But she and her husband hired *me* to run this hospital and that's what I intend to do."

Maddie snorted. "You think I need my mother to get your job?"

He drummed his fingers on the desk, his eyes raking her from the top of her head to the soles of her feet. "I thought southern girls were supposed to be sweet and easy to get along with."

She didn't like the way his gaze cut straight through her bravado. "Oh, we can be sweet, but don't turn your back on us for a minute."

"Then I guess it behooves me to keep my enemies close."

"Behooves?" Maddie couldn't hold back a laugh. "Who says behooves?"

The return of his cocky smirk produced symmetrical dimples. "Tell you what, Dr. Harper, have dinner with me tonight and I'll go over all the big words in your contract."

If he wasn't so condescending, she'd accuse him of hitting on her. "We can discuss my contract right here, right now."

"I'm in this hospital fifteen hours a day. I need some fresh air."

She could stand here and argue about the multitude of ethical lines he'd crossed and probably win her case, but what she wanted was the ability to guarantee Parker's recovery. "Name the time and place, *Chief.*" She ground his title as an emphatic reminder of the professional standards that came with his position.

"There's a new steak place on the lake."

"I'd rather stay close to the hospital."

He sighed, "That just leaves the Koffee Kup."

"Don't look so glum," Maddie said smugly. "Friday night is all-you-can-eat fried catfish." She wheeled for the door.

"Until we have a signed agreement," he called after her. "No practicing medicine in my hospital."

She stopped and spun on her heels. "Does *your* hospital also have rules against sitting with a friend?"

"In quarantine, yes."

She answered him with a glare. "See you at seven." Without waiting for his agreement, she marched from his office feeling equally victorious and apprehensive.

A few hours later, Maddie peered over the nurse's shoulder for a sneak peek at the computer. The speed at which Parker's lab numbers had improved was a thrill greater than any she'd had during her infectious disease fellowship. Seeing what she'd learned actually save a life proved she'd chosen the right course.

Maddie waited until the nurse left the room then dug her stethoscope from her backpack. She plastered the bell to Parker's hairy chest. "No crackling of the lung bases. Abdominal distension drastically reduced. Fever not gone, but abating." If this course of antibiotics continued doing its work, Parker could avoid the complications she'd been dreading. She raised her head and eyed him soberly.

Concern narrowed Parker's eyes. "Well?"

"Typhoid kills over twenty million people a year." She folded her stethoscope, relishing the concern on Parker's face. "You aren't going to be one of them."

"Don't look so disappointed." The strength in Parker's voice pleased her nearly as much as her proper diagnosis and treatment.

She slipped the stethoscope into her backpack. Parker's olive complexion showed none of the yellowing signs of jaundice. Dark stubble shadowed his square chin. His mop of dark curls needed a trim, or at the very least a good shampoo and a comb. He was thinner than he'd been at Momma's wedding, but his eyes, dark and flecked with gold, could still see into her soul. She squirmed ever so slightly. The shift broke the hold his gaze had on her. "Is there someone we should call?"

"My parents."

"Besides Kathy and Ryan."

His eyes slid to the window. "When can I get out of here?"

Instead of addressing his change of subject with the head-on inquiry a secret child deserved, she took a different tactic. "I know you're feeling better, but I'd like you to complete a short, five-day course of antibiotics. Once your blood and stool cultures are sterile, you'll be free to return to your ranch or roam the jungles of Guatemala." She should leave her answer there, professional and succinct, but she couldn't. "Except you're not free, are you?"

He gaze whipped back to her. "No."

"Shouldn't you call Isabella's mother?"

"Easier said than done."

"The woman's entitled to know that you've taken her child to America, and that she's okay."

"Don't tell me how to raise my daughter."

"Why are you being so shady about Isabella? That's not like you. Did you sleep with Gabriella and have to—"

"Whoa." His raised palm told her she'd crossed the line. "How do you know Gabriella is Isabella's mother?"

Her eyes darted toward the phone on his tray table. "I . . . I might have seen your screensaver and put two and two together."

He snatched his phone. "Last time we talked, you made it pretty clear you would live your life, and that I should live mine." He waggled his phone. "My life. My business."

"You know, my initial prognosis might have been wrong." She crossed her arms. "Your condition has obviously progressed to a paranoid psychosis because last I checked, we may have gone our separate ways, but I thought we'd parted as friends."

"Friends keep in touch."

"You could have texted me." Her phone vibrated in her pocket. She pulled it out, her heart thumping in protest to his accusations, "Hey, Momma."

"Dr. Boyer is wondering where you are."

"Shoot!" Maddie glanced at the wall clock. Seven fifteen. "I forgot all about him.

"You won't get a second chance to make a good first impression. There are limits to my influence."

"I'm proof of that, aren't I?" Maddie clicked off her phone. "I've got to go, Parker."

His head fell back on the pillow. "So, what else is new?"

She let herself get lost for a moment in those deep, dark eyes. But the warmth had been replaced with a cool distance. Shaking off the chill seeping into her bones, she said, "Don't try getting out of that bed on your own."

"You'd be amazed what all I've learned to do on my own. I think I can handle a few steps to the john."

"Maybe, but if you fall, then you've got to handle me…and you've never been able to do that."

He didn't smile at her teasing. "Guess that fancy doctor's fixin' to find out he can't handle you either."

Hard headedness had carried her through life as a preacher's kid, the disadvantages of graduating from a small Christian college, the exhausting demands of med school, and her mother's constant attempts to plan her life. Had her heart hardened, too? "Promise me you'll give yourself a couple of days to rest and recover, okay, Parker?"

"You promise to get me back to my little girl sooner rather than later, and I promise not to bother you again." He rolled over and faced the window, leaving her with no choice but to charge toward her next battle.

CHAPTER SIX

Maddie whipped into the parking slot beside the shiny black convertible. She ripped the ponytail holder from her hair and fluffed her curls. She flipped open the mirror on her sun visor and dragged a swipe of lip gloss across her lips. The effort was more than the arrogant Dr. Boyer deserved, but some of her Texas roots were too deep to yank. Any southern girl worth her salt was well-practiced in the art of winning more flies with honey, which was the only reason she hadn't given Parker the tongue-lashing he deserved. She and Parker would never be lovers, but she was determined to help her oldest and dearest friend get back on his feet…whether he wanted her help or not. And if helping Parker find his way back to their friendship meant acting a southern-girl-fool to gain hospital privileges from the bottom-feeder she was meeting for dinner, then so be it.

Stepping inside the diner was like stepping back in time. A time Maddie hadn't revisited since her daddy's death. The jangle of the bell above the door jarred loose memories of her father marching her up to the counter, plopping her on one of the bar stools, and spinning her until the world blurred. The aroma of fried fish and stout coffee joined the sting of unshed tears. She stopped at the *Please Wait to Be Seated* sign.

"Be right with you, Maddie." Ruthie, the diner's owner, lumbered out from behind the counter. Ruthie's hair, now almost as white as the crisp apron cinched around her expanding middle, was pulled back in the same teased-up French twist she'd worn since the 50's. "Didn't expect your Momma to let you miss a meal at her table."

"I'm meeting Dr. Boyer."

Ruthie's brows crept higher, then her eyes cut to the back booth where Dr. Boyer waited, impatience deepening fine lines at the corner of his eyes. "No wonder he's been watchin' the door like a horny bull waitin' on the gate to be left open."

Maddie swallowed a snicker at a saying she hadn't heard in years and decided she'd enjoy making the arrogant man wait a little longer. She nodded toward the welcome sign. "This new?"

"Angus had it installed before he left." Ruthie pulled a menu from a wooden rack by the cash register. "The boy thought it would speed up our service and add a touch of class to the joint."

"Your grandson still making his special brownies?"

Ruthie chuckled at Maddie's mention of the Christmas service and the marijuana-laced treats that had made Momma and Maxine higher than kites. "He learnt a good lesson on that one. He's decided to stay out of the kitchen. Been studying business at that fancy college you went to in Abilene." A proud grin reached Ruthie's tired eyes. "Graduates with honors this Saturday."

"Good for him."

Ruthie leaned in close and whispered, "Wouldn't have happened if a couple of *someones* we both know and love hadn't seen what I saw in the boy and paid his way."

Ruthie's gratitude was a pinprick to Maddie's conscience. Saul and Momma had done so much with the windfall of Daddy's investments and people loved them for it. "Hope you're closing the diner and going to Abilene to help him celebrate."

"Wouldn't miss it for the world. Your momma and Saul offered to drive me." Ruthie's eyes cut to the back booth where Dr. Boyer was suddenly very focused on the menu. "Don't know why Mr. Too-big-for-his-britches is botherin' to read the specials. He orders the same thing every time. Steak and a dry baked potato."

"Better get me over there before he does something crazy."

Ruthie grabbed a menu from the wooden rack. "Like order the catfish?"

"I was thinking a hamburger with the works."

Ruthie shook her head and lowered her voice again, "Supposedly, his only vice is fast women."

"I know for certain he likes fast cars."

"You don't say." A sly grin tugged the corners of Ruthie's lips. "I think you and that little red thing you're drivin' can take him easy enough." She handed Maddie a menu. "Please tell me our Parker's going to pull through."

"The Story sisters activated the prayer chain, didn't they?"

Ruthie snorted. "The twin treasures would never let something as dangerous as a tropical disease go unchallenged by the Lord." Ruthie's faith was surprisingly enviable.

"I've said all I can say about my patient, Ruthie."

The diner owner's eyes narrowed. "I thought we were talkin' about your *friend,* not just another patient."

Were they still friends? From the way Parker was refusing to talk to her about Isabella or anything else that mattered, it felt as if she'd lost her friend. For good.

"Let's get this showdown on the road," Maddie whispered.

As Ruthie worked her way across the diner, pushing in chairs and straightening napkin holders, Maddie was once again reminded how hard it was to keep anything private in this town.

Ruthie straightened at Dr. Boyer's booth. "Here's the rest of your party, doc." She whipped out the towel tucked in the back of her apron and swatted away the crumbs on the empty bench seat across from the doctor dressed in a crisp blue button-down and expensive red silk tie.

"Thank you, Ruthie." In an unexpected gesture of gallantry, Dr. Boyer scooted from his seat, stood, and extended his hand. "Thanks for agreeing to conduct business after hours, Dr. Harper." If Maddie hadn't Googled the man, she might not have known his emphasis on *conduct business* was as much an effort to protect his reputation from the Mt. Hope rumor mill as her own.

"I always enjoy a good burger and a chocolate shake." Maddie shook his hand with the confident grip her father had taught her, then slid into the seat. "Sorry I'm late. Traffic." She'd never been good at joking and from the lack of amusement in his incredibly blue eyes she hadn't improved in that area. "Okay, I got caught up—"

"Holding your sick friend's hand, right?"

"Right." Knowing he'd kept tabs on her made her a little unsettled. "I'll have my usual please, Ruthie."

The seasoned waitress frowned. "We'll see how you do on the burger and shake before I bring out the pie." Ruthie looked at the doctor. "You havin' *your* usual, doc?"

He handed his menu to Ruthie. "I think I'll have what Dr. Harper's having tonight."

If Ruthie was surprised by the doctor's order, she kept her poker face. "How do you want that burger cooked?"

"Any way you decide will be perfect, Ruthie," he said with a wink.

Now he'd gone too far. Oozing charm all over her was part of this cat and mouse game they were playing. Pretending he was charmed by Ruthie was . . . well, it was maddening, that's what it was.

Maddie bit her tongue, waiting until Ruthie had the shake machine whirring too loudly to overhear the tongue-lashing she intended to give this guy. "Learn your charm practicing in Dallas, Dr. Boyer?"

His fixed stare was a laser. "You could have blamed your lack of punctuality on the New York or Washington subway system."

This guy was no one's fool. "Okay," she admitted. "We've Googled each other."

Eyes still honed on hers, he carefully unrolled his silverware from the paper napkin. "Then you're probably wondering why a maternal-fetal specialist would leave a high-profile, lucrative practice for a start-up program in an underfunded and poorly equipped West Texas hospital?"

"I'm not wondering."

His smug smile melted. "If you should decide to practice medicine rather than sit behind a microscope at the CDC…" His eyes became surprisingly transparent, clear of any attempt to hide the huge lawsuit and the ugly media coverage that had followed his misdiagnosis of a high-profile woman's pregnancy complications. "…you'll learn that the first patient lost on your table sticks with you."

Unexpected compassion at his honesty deflated her plan to threaten him with exposure if he didn't grant her wishes. "I don't think anybody avoids those first-year mistakes."

"From what I've seen, you're pretty sharp, Dr. Harper. Bringing Parker Kemp home was a good call."

This was not at all how she expected this conversation to go. "Does that mean I have privileges?"

"Full."

"Don't you have to run it past the board?"

"Done."

"Apparently you make executive decisions as fast as you drive."

The corner of his lip raised in a half-smile. "The board is a generous group of men and women who believe in giving everyone a chance." He didn't say *second* chance, but from the change in his demeanor she got the impression he considered coming to Mt.

Hope an opportunity he did not take for granted. "Hometown girl was an easy sell."

"Funny how one person's hell can be another person's heaven."

He ripped a napkin from the holder then mopped condensation from his water glass. "I take it fighting for hospital privileges in Mt. Hope wasn't high on your bucket list."

"Kicking the bucket would have been preferable to practicing medicine in this one-horse town."

"Want me to deny your request?"

"Trust me, neither of us want to explain that one to Momma."

"Leona Levy's a remarkable woman. Her contributions keep us one step ahead of our creditors."

"I didn't realize Momma was carrying the hospital's entire financial burden—"

"No one does."

"Ah. Loose lips sink ships, right?"

"People don't want to drive to bigger cities for their medical care, but they will if they get spooked. An understaffed and out-of-date facility puts lives at risk."

Feeling the need to offer an olive branch, she said, "I can work the family clinic for free—"

"Get your patient past the danger zone, and then we'll work out your clinic schedule and pay scale."

Men never came out and said she was too pushy, too smart, too intimidating… they just walked away. Why wasn't Robin Boyer following suit? "I've been monitoring Parker's labs and adjusting his treatment accordingly."

Dr. Boyer didn't seem the least bit surprised or put off by her assertive actions. Her confession, in fact, raised the corner of his lip again, this time in pleased interest. "And?"

"He'll live…if I don't kill him first."

"Sounds like you two have…history. You sure you can keep your feelings out of the treatment mix?"

"He kissed me."

Robin cocked a brow. "Before or after you hopped a plane to Guatemala?"

"It was in second grade."

"First love sticks with a person longer than losing your first patient."

"Parker's sudden display of affection was simply an overreaction to a bike wreck. An emotional response to my bloody ankle. Hardly a first-love scenario."

"Then why did he come to your defense today?"

Why had he? "We grew up together. We were best friends."

"Were?" His raised brows implied there was more to the story.

Even if there had been more to the story of Maddie and Parker—which she'd made sure there never had been—she knew better than to let her guard down. Why had she told this man about the ridiculous kiss a boy had given her years ago?

She was in the middle of mentally searching for a small-talk diversion when Ruthie showed up with two steaming plates and a couple of frothy shakes.

"Burgers. Medium well. Condiments on the side." Ruthie set the frosty mugs before them. "Y'all don't start in on me about needin' pie until these plates are clean. You hear?"

Dr. Boyer stared at the huge mound of curly potatoes and the slab of charred meat on a Texas-sized bun. "Like the sign says, folks are as generous as the dust here in Mt. Hope." He smiled at Maddie. "Last one done with their burger buys the pie."

"You don't have to eat all of that."

"And you could have secured hospital privileges without agreeing to the clinic work." He grabbed the ketchup bottle. "It's not so bad here, you know?"

"Wait until all this beef plugs your arteries."

He took a bite and rolled his eyes in delight. "Definitely worth a heart cath."

He had a point. She'd been so busy searching the horizon for her future she'd failed to consider the things she loved about her past...like having a restaurant owner know her name and what she liked to eat before she ever opened her mouth. What a strange feeling to see her hometown through the eyes of newcomer.

Maddie lifted her shake mug. "To the advancement of modern medicine, Dr. Boyer."

He picked up his mug and accepted her toast. "Robin."

"Maddie." She smiled as their mugs clinked.

Momma was wrong. A girl could catch flies with honesty.

CHAPTER SEVEN

Maddie hurried through the quiet hospital halls, her step lightened by how well her meeting had gone with Dr. Boyer. She'd misjudged Mt. Hope's new chief of staff by more than the miles his convertible had put between them. Besides being ridiculously handsome, he was smart, fair, and obviously not intimidated by her abilities. She couldn't wait to tell Parker that, thanks to Dr. Boyer, he was stuck with her until he was well enough to be released.

She barreled around the corner and nearly collided with the tall beauty knocking on Parker's door. "Nellie?"

Maxine's startled daughter turned. It took her only a millisecond to take in the woman who'd caught her trying to breech the quarantine sign. "Maddie. You look great." She wrapped Maddie in a brief, overly perfumed hug. "Mom said you saved Parker's life."

Nellie had matured into a knockout. Short shorts accented her long legs, and the seductive off-the-shoulder top accented her motive.

Suddenly conscious of her dirty scrubs, Maddie crossed her arms over her chest. "Maxine told me you were…"—she paused and choked back a sudden and surprising wave of jealousy—"*helping* Kathy take care of Parker's ranch while I take care of Parker."

Nellie waved off Maddie's jab as if it had been offered as praise. "There's so much to do, especially now with Ryan pushing a walker and Kathy working night and day to help that sweet baby adjust." Feline-shaped green eyes offset Nellie's creamy complexion. Calm and concern sparkled in her unusually demure expression. "Isn't Isabella just the cutest thing you've ever seen? Busy, but so cute." Nellie's mane of silky amber hair reminded Maddie that a fire was always burning just below Nellie's sugary smile.

All she had to do was poke at the embers and this whole I-care-so-much façade would go up in smoke. "She's beautiful."

"She keeps asking for her *Paki*…" Nellie let her questions trail off, her cat-like eyes evaluating Maddie's willingness to slip her information as her long fingers toyed with the thin gold chain at her neck. Maddie smiled, hoping her silence would end the conversation. Instead, Nellie pressed on, "Well, anyway, I promised the cute little thing I'd come to town and check on her daddy, maybe let her facetime him for a quick second."

Maddie pointed to the KEEP OUT sign on the door. "I'm afraid seeing Parker is out of the question."

"Surely that silly quarantine doesn't include friends who are caring for his family. Right, Mads?"

She did not like hearing Parker's nickname for her rolling off Nellie's forked tongue any more than she liked having her professional opinion discounted…an opinion she'd worked hard to perfect. "Everyone."

"Then how are *you* getting in?"

"I'm his doctor."

"Not his wife." Nellie tilted her head, her eyes taking in Maddie's scrubs and disheveled appearance. "But I guess it pays to have connections."

"Pays to go to school for years and work your tail off." Success with Dr. Boyer had made her bold, but from the narrowing of Nellie's eyes, it had also made her reckless.

"Just because *you* don't want Parker doesn't mean no one else does."

"I don't know what you're talking about."

"The preacher's daughter has always believed she was entitled to the attentions of every man within a hundred-mile radius. But as soon as any of these men get too close, you move on. Where's it going to stop?"

"Nellie, you should go."

"My mother drove by the diner and saw you having dinner with Dr. Boyer." She leaned in close enough to smell her breath mint. "You can't just waltz back into Mt. Hope and scoop up the only available bachelor between here and civilization *and* keep your claws in the sweetest man who ever lived."

Small towns. Big gossips. Ugh. Another reason she couldn't wait to get to Atlanta. "I didn't know you'd laid claim to Mt. Hope Memorial's chief of staff."

Nellie swung her purse over her bare shoulder. "You'll move on. Not soon enough, but you will. You always do. And when you're gone, I'll be here to pick up the pieces."

Maddie returned Nellie's smug smile. "Doctor or cowboy?"

"I'm not as picky as some." Nellie wheeled then her long legs carried her toward the exit with the stealthy strut of a lioness.

Normally, Maddie would be thrilled that she'd sent the girl back to her lair. But she knew Nellie far too well. This fiery-haired tiger would regroup then return to the game with her bent-out-of-shape claws sharpened and ready for the perfect moment to pounce.

Maddie took a moment to let her elevated blood pressure idle back to normal. Why should she care who Nellie pursued? Or what tricks she'd employ to ensnare them? Nellie's accusations of

Maddie's intentions to capture the attention of every guy who even looked at her were unfounded during their teenager years, and they were completely off track now. Maddie didn't want every guy that came along.

She only wanted Parker.

The thought hit her harder than if Nellie had hauled off and slapped her.

Air squeezing from her lungs, Maddie turned from Parker's door and started toward the opposite exit. She didn't want Parker, or a life of hiking boots and sacrifice. She wanted heels and financial security. She barreled toward the stairwell door and a place to think.

Halfway down the hall the elevator dinged. Her brother stepped out and Maddie stopped. "David, what are you doing here?"

"Visiting the sick."

"It's well past visiting hours," she snapped. "Do I need to instruct the Story sisters to notify the prayer chain that *no one* can see Parker? Not even the pastor?"

"I came to see you."

"I'm not sick."

"Can't a brother check on his sister?"

"If you've come to bug me again about making room in my overloaded schedule for a family dinner, you're wasting your time. I'm not going to feel guilty for working my tail off or putting in the extra hours."

"We've hardly seen you since you roared into town."

She set her feet. "Parker's not out of the woods yet."

His eyes cut toward Parker's door. "There's a fine line between helping and hurting."

"Nellie tattled on me, didn't she?"

The same impish grin he used to give her every time she'd nailed him on racking up another of grandmother's under-the-table gifts curled the corner of his lips. "She might have sent me a couple of seething texts."

"Something to the effect of *make Maddie stop thinking she can have every guy that's breathing.*"

"Okay." He took her arm. "Somebody needs coffee."

"I just had dinner."

"Robin's a nice guy."

"Did Nellie text you about him, too?"

He smiled at her rising ire, which only made her angrier. "Robin and I shoot hoops a couple of times a week at the gym. He may have mentioned that you weren't nearly as mean as I'd made you out to be."

She shook her head, marveling more at the change in her older brother than the lack of privacy in this small town. David had always been the smart one. She'd become a doctor to prove he wasn't the only one with brains in the family. Like him, she'd left Mt. Hope two minutes after turning in her high school cap and gown. But David had been so intent on ensuring a future so different than their parents, he'd gone a step further and studied abroad. And yet, here he was. Living in the house where they'd grown up. Preaching from the pulpit their father had filled for years. Married with two kids. And completely content with his choice to come home.

Her eyes narrowed. "This town will never need surveillance cameras as long as the gossips are alive and well."

"The trick to throwing off the busybodies is to give them something juicy, but benign, to talk about. Keeps them busy while you do what you really want." Putting his teasing aside, David's face softened. "Momma said you were meeting Robin to hash out the terms of your ability to care for Parker."

"It's settled."

"How does Parker feel about having you so close?"

"I haven't told him."

"Because?"

"Because I don't want him to think there's more to my hospital-privileges campaign than simply that he's sick and I'm an infectious disease specialist."

Relief registered on David's face. "Parker's a smart guy. He'll get it if you tell him the truth."

"If I wanted your advice, I would've asked for it."

"Since when?" David kissed her cheek. "Just promise me you won't be stupid and give my friend hope where there is none." David wheeled.

"He's my friend, too," she shouted at her brother's back.

"That ship sailed when you went east, and Parker went south," he lobbed the truth over his shoulder and into her court. "Both of you were too stubborn to call." He left her standing in an empty hallway with nothing but accusations to consider.

Why couldn't men and women just be friends? Parker made her laugh. She made him think. He helped her lighten up. She helped him buckle down. He would never have gotten around to going to Guatemala if…if she hadn't…what?

Left him.

The truth was another hammer blow to her heart. David was right. Real friends don't run away.

Gut heavy with the need to apologize to Parker and to prove to herself that she and the guy she'd known since first grade could be friends again, she went to Parker's door and knocked lightly.

"It's open." The strength in her patient's voice prickled her skin.

She stepped inside. "It better not be. You're in quarantine." She was pleased to see Parker sitting up in bed and jabbing a spoon at the dinner tray in front of him.

"Feels more like I'm suffering one of those time-outs Mom used to give me whenever I let bugs loose in my room to see which ones ate the corn." He pointed to a bowl of melted Jell-O. "Bet your dinner was better than mine."

A healthier color peeked from beneath the dark stubble on his face. He'd showered. His unruly mop was dark and slicked back, curling above the neck of his hospital gown. His eyes were clearer, grateful, and studying her carefully. Guatemala had hardened his muscles and softened his soul. A disturbingly attractive combination.

"Dinner was better than I expected." Maddie ventured closer. "Juicy burger. Salty, hot fries." She taunted him with the seductive licking of her lips. "Frosty chocolate shake. It was classic Ruthie at her finest."

"Your bedside manner has not improved." He dropped his spoon on his tray. "You know the nurses call you the Wicked Witch of the west wing, right?"

She raised her hands and cupped her fingers into claws. "Come here, my pretty." When he didn't laugh at her Wizard of Oz imitation, she pushed his bedside table clear of his reach and stepped closer. "Lucky for you, I'm the witch who's going to have you eating more of Ruthie's burgers and fries than you can stand in a few weeks."

He snorted and shook his head. "Another one bites the dust."

"What does that mean?"

"Dr. Boyer caved, didn't he?"

"Caved?"

"Boyer may look like a Greek god, but it's good to know he's a mere mortal after all... just like the rest of us poor suckers."

She stiffened. "What are you talking about?"

"Don't pretend you didn't know that all you had to do was bat those killer lashes of yours and you'd get your way."

She perched on the side of his bed. Tempted as she was to put a kink in the line running to his IV pole, she reeled in her anger. She'd always known cutting him loose would hurt him badly. Seeing the pain he still carried was something altogether different. "I'm sorry I haven't called since we, you know, went our separate ways." She wanted to reach for him, to offer vague excuses, but he deserved for her to keep her distance as much as he deserved the truth. "I was scared," she whispered.

"Of what?"

"Everything." The time for vague excuses had passed. "Of becoming my mother."

"Do I look like your dad?"

She smiled. "You could be his clone…not physically…although you're both big as a mountain…but you think like him. What mattered to him matters to you." She ticked off her list. "Faith. Family. Frugality."

"And that's bad because…?"

"Because his ideals killed him."

"I thought he died of a heart attack."

"Broken heart…from years and years of serving this broken world and getting nothing back."

He let out a long, slow breath. "Your dad loved ministry."

"You don't know the stress."

"I'm sorry it was hard…on him, your mom, you."

"When he left us, it nearly killed my mother. I can't do that…be left with nothing to fall back on."

"I'm not going to die."

"You almost did."

Parker held up his palm in truce. "I'm sorry I didn't tell you about Isabella. I wanted to call but I didn't think you'd want to listen."

Without any hesitation, she linked fingers with him. His grip was calloused from four years of manual labor, but his hand swallowed hers with the same security she'd always felt in his presence. "I'm listening now."

He squeezed her hand in a show of gratitude for her support. "You remember Gabriella?"

Maddie's stomach sunk. "The pretty clinic nurse from South Texas?"

Parker nodded. "She and I became good friends." Did his pause imply he'd wanted more? "Very good friends. And—"

"You know, it's really none of my business who you…" She tried to pull away from the burn between their palms, but he wouldn't let her go.

"No, it's not like that." He laughed at her distraught face. "You're jealous, aren't you?"

"I'm concerned."

"Concerned?" he pressed, squeezing harder.

"Okay, I'll admit to curious."

"Curious?"

"As to what kind of girl Parker Kemp would *befriend*."

"You know what kind." His gaze held her tight as his grip.

She shook her head slowly. "Parker, we're just—"

"Friends. Same as always." He eased his hold, releasing her as easily as he'd let her go four years earlier. "You really need to work on your bedside manner."

She didn't have the heart to tell him lab rats didn't expect her to babysit their emotions. "Don't change the subject."

He looked at her, weighing the risks, then slowly began to wade back into her confidence. "Gabby and I hung out a lot…until this new doctor from Brazil came to do a stint at the clinic. Perez was a great guy. We all liked him, but it didn't take a rocket scientist to figure out that with Perez on the scene, Gabby and I would never be more than friends. I'm not as slow as I used to be at spotting the signs." His pause was a peek into the hurt she'd inflicted and didn't know how to heal. "Gabby fell in love with Perez. They married quickly, and had Isabella ten months later. They asked me to be her godfather."

"Isabella's not *your* daughter." Maddie couldn't believe the relief pumping through her veins.

A shadow passed over Parker's face. "She is now."

"Are you going to help me make the puzzle pieces fit or leave me to guess how this happened?"

"Three weeks ago, Perez had to make an early morning run up the mountain to help deliver a baby for a woman who'd labored all night. If he had to do a C-section, he'd need help. So, Gabby agreed to go along. They were only going to be gone a couple of hours. I offered to watch Isabella."

Parker swallowed and Maddie felt her own body stiffen as he prepared to deliver the rest of the story. "By nightfall, I knew something was wrong." His gaze drifted past her and, from the tears forming in his eyes, crashed smack into a painful memory. "I left Isabella with Flory, the woman I rented a room from, and went looking for them. I didn't find them until the next morning." He swiped his eyes. "You remember how perilous some of those switchbacks can be, right?"

"Oh no," Maddie whispered, both dreading the heartbreaking details of what he found and desperate to hear them.

His watery gaze searched hers for the strength to speak. "Their jeep had been swept down the mountain by a mudslide."

Her heart broke for the young love snuffed out so early and for their precious daughter orphaned in an instant. "I'm so sorry, Parker."

"We all were." He let out another pained sigh. "Anyway, once I got past the shock of losing my friends, I realized something had to be done about Isabella."

"So, you volunteered to raise her?"

He shook his head. "I wasn't even married. How could I be a father?"

"Then why did you…"

"You know how the clinic hounds any American staffer or volunteer to stay current on their paperwork?"

"Yes."

"When Gabby and Perez made their will, they asked me if I'd also serve as Isabella's legal guardian. I agreed…I mean, what were the odds the need would ever come up, right? After all, they were young and healthy and…so in love."

She and Parker stared at each other. Neither speaking. Love didn't protect people from hurt.

Maddie swallowed back tears. "But surely Gabriella's family or someone in Perez's family would want her."

Parker shook his head. "Sadly, neither of them had another soul in the world. Loneliness was the thing that drew Gabby and Perez together."

Common ground. The glue for any relationship. She and Parker were oil and water. They were about as opposite as two people could possibly be. She'd been a fool to entertain the possibility they could even be good friends. "But—"

"I did some pretty-quick soul searching. Was going to call my parents to talk it through with them, but before I had the chance, Mom called me crying. She was so upset about Dad's injury. I didn't have the heart to break news like this over the phone. I planned to tell her when I brought Isabella home. I knew the minute she saw that beautiful little girl, she'd agree that I'd made the right decision."

"Decision?"

His eyes, now clear and resolute, no longer asked for understanding. "I'm all Isabella's got. And I'm going to raise her like she's all mine."

"Adopt her?"

He nodded. "After I get the legalities sorted."

"Are you sure? This is a big step?"

"Is it so hard to imagine me as a father?"

Frankly, it wasn't. He'd always had a way with kids. The summer they were junior high camp counselors, the kids had lined up to be on Parker's team. Her face sobered. "You're over twenty-five. Somewhat mentally stable. And don't have a known criminal background. Isabella could do far worse." She smiled wanly at her pitiful attempt to lighten the situation with a joke.

"You're forgetting my most important qualification."

"What's that?"

"I never give up…especially on love."

His pointed gaze was an arrow straight through her heart. "How are you going to do this?"

"Raise a child without a wife?"

"Yes."

"Lots of people are single parents. The Lord has called me to father this little girl. I'm counting on Him to give me the strength and wisdom."

"I know you, Parker Kemp. You've had your heart set on a wife, two kids, and a white picket fence since you were ten."

"Nine," he said with a stubborn lift to his chin.

That Parker would selflessly reverse his course for the good of this child was so…like him. Some women might have found this quality attractive. Endearing. Possibly even sexy. But she was aggravated. Mad to the core. Mad that he'd never once volunteered to give up everything for her.

But then she'd never pushed him into a corner and asked him. Friends didn't make selfish demands on friends.

Why not? Because she knew this friend would do everything within his power to make her happy. Parker would walk away from everything he held dear to follow her to the ends of the earth.

Everything but his faith. And now his daughter. And without either of them, he wouldn't be the Parker Kemp she loved. She could never ask him to be less than he was. And she knew he cared enough to never ask the same of her.

She conceded with a small nod and an even smaller smile. "You're not made of special dust, you know. This is going to be hard."

"I'm not the one afraid of hard."

CHAPTER EIGHT

Two days later, Maddie had successfully transferred her credentials, verified her shot record, and secured a pair of Mt. Hope Memorial scrubs. She twisted her hair into a tight knot and slid her arms into the new white coat Dr. Boyer had expedited on her behalf. Above the upper right pocket, he'd had it monogrammed with *Madison Harper, MD, Internal Medicine*. The left pocket sported the new hospital logo that Momma's generous contributions had bought her the right to design. Maddie dragged her finger over the embroidered red heart impaled by a gold cross. The image reminded her of how the stress of church work had broken her father's heart. Did Momma feel the same? Discovering Momma's true feelings about anything would require them to have a real conversation.

Maddie pushed away the futile longing to really know her mother, draped her stethoscope around her neck, then stepped into the shiny hall of the new Harper Memorial wing. According to the overhead signage, the family clinic and the chapel were down the hall to her right.

Chapel?

With no desire to set foot inside a chapel, Maddie hurried along the corridor. She ground to an abrupt halt at the two stone pillars flanking a large wooden door. The familiar colonial-style entry looked out of place against the sleek tiled walls and glistening marble floors. Had someone stolen the old front door to Mt. Hope Community Church?

She took a cautious step toward the bronze plaque bolted to the wall.

James David Harper Memorial Chapel.

Maddie swallowed hard. Surely Momma hadn't replicated the scene of Daddy's death in the middle of a place that was supposed to offer life? Had Momma also recreated the church's interior? Complete with Daddy's larger-than-life pulpit?

Heart pounding frantically, Maddie wrapped her fingers around the brass door handle. Just as she was about to pull the door open, someone cleared their throat behind her. Startled, she turned her head.

A bruised woman sat in a wheelchair, her casted leg sticking out in front of her. "Have you come for prayer, doctor?"

Maddie released the handle. "No." She wheeled. As she marched toward the nurses' station at the far end of the hall, she could feel the woman's confused gaze following her escape.

Freda Stringer, a salt and pepper, no-nonsense fence post who'd taught Maddie's junior high Sunday school class, stood with her hands on her hips. "Dr. Boyer told me to expect you." Disapproval of the temporary arrangement simmered in the nurse's voice.

Could her luck get any worse? Freda the Stringer-upper, as she and David used to call her behind her back, had never been a champion of the pastor's kids. From her current scowl, Maddie's success at becoming a doctor had not improved her opinion.

"Mrs. Stringer." Maddie held out her hand. "What a surprise. It's good to see you."

"*Nurse* Stringer." Freda nodded toward the hand sanitizer on the counter. "We open at eight."

"Sorry," Maddie stuttered as she pumped clear liquid into her palm. "Had to sign a bunch of forms for HR and then get my white coat from—"

"As you can see—" Freda waved a wrinkled hand at the full waiting room. "—you'll have to hoof it to catch up."

"Good thing I ate my Wheaties this morning."

Freda was not amused. She handed Maddie a thin file and pointed to a door labeled Exam Room One. "Possible acute otitis media."

Only a month. I can do anything for a month. Even middle ear infections. Even Freda.

"On it." Maddie took a deep breath and strode to the closed exam door. Trying to recall proper treatment options if the eardrum had been perforated, she flipped to the first page of the chart. Her stomach dropped.

A child.

Her first diagnostic exam to administer in over a year, and she'd drawn a *child.* Either she was suffering from the worst luck in the world or God had a spiteful sense of humor. Maddie could feel Freda's eyes burning a hole in her back. She wasn't about to give this woman the satisfaction of chalking up another black mark on her attendance chart.

Maddie lightly rapped the door. "Good morning," she chirped as she bustled into the room.

A worried mother held her nine-month-old boy in her lap. The moment Maddie extended her hand, the kid burst into an ear-piercing wail. If his eardrum wasn't ruptured, it would be now. Three minutes later, Maddie emerged from the exam room with curdled formula splattered across her monogrammed name, perspiration soaking the pits of her white coat, and a pounding headache.

She glanced at the nurses' station where Freda held out another chart. "Projectile vomiting. First grader. Room two."

It was nearly three in the afternoon when Maddie's growling stomach reminded her that she'd not had time for lunch because of all the runny noses and low electrolytes. She peeked into the waiting room. No more little people. "I'm going to pop over to the cafeteria," she told Freda with a weary sigh. That she wasn't planning on coming back was information she kept to herself.

Freda shook her head. "The patients in room three have been here thirty minutes. They insist they're staying until they see you."

Maddie held back the tart responses lined up on her tongue. She wasn't about to let anyone torpedo her ability to care for Parker. She'd work around the clock, and examine a hundred children if that was what it was going to take to keep her hand in his care.

"Bring 'em on." Maddie snatched the chart from Freda's hand. Blood pressure boiling, she burst into the exam room and ground to a surprised stop. "Etta May? Nola Gay?" Maddie dug out the smile this day had long since buried and gave them each a hug. "Finally, someone over two foot tall." She dropped onto the rolling exam stool. "What brings y'all in today?"

Nola Gay clutched the handles of a shiny black pocketbook, her face more serious than usual. "Sister's not feeling well."

"Tell her the truth, Sister," Etta May scolded, her swollen ankles dangling from her perch atop the exam table. She rested one arm on what looked like a picnic basket trimmed in checkered cloth.

"We came to help," Nola Gay pointed at the suitcase sitting in the corner. Not the modern kind with wheels, but a giant, faded, red vinyl one that had been in the attic so long its handles had cracked from the heat and the color had become a splotchy pink.

"Help?" Maddie was confused. "Who? Me?"

"Not you." Etta May shifted on the crunchy white paper covering the examination couch. "You're very competent."

"I wish someone would tell Freda."

"Freda's probably just suffering from a little professional jealousy because your mother goes on and on about how brilliant you are all the time," Nola Gay said.

"She does?" Maddie regretted the way her surprise quickly raised the old girls' gossip antennas.

"Oh yes, sweet thang." Etta May nodded. "She's very proud of you, as are we. Right, Sister?"

Nola Gay peered over her glasses, studying Maddie for the slightest twitch. "Right."

Maddie kept her face a blank slate. "Good to know."

"Tell Maddie your brilliant idea, Sister," Etta May encouraged. "Nola's always been the smart one."

"Wait," Maddie interrupted. "Are either of you sick?"

"Oh, well that's what we've come to talk about," Etta May continued. "Go on Nola Gay, tell her."

Nola Gay drew her purse close to her abundant chest. "We heard the hospital is suffering a cash flow problem."

"Maybe you need to talk to Momma," Maddie said. "She's on the board. Not me."

Nola Gay shook her head. "We need *you* to help *us* help the hospital stay in the black."

"I wouldn't know anything about the hospital's finances."

"Of course, you wouldn't. You've been busy gettin' the medical education that is going to save our dear Parker," Etta May said. "And we are all ever so grateful. Right, Sister?"

Nola Gay nodded, "We've heard our handsome little extension agent is coming along nicely?" Nola Gay's statement was more of a question that plied Maddie for added information.

For the sake of abiding by HIPPA rules, Maddie knew to keep her answer as prayer-chain-gossip-free as possible. "He is."

Etta May's brows rose hopefully. "Coming along?"

Nola Gay pressed forward in her seat. "Or handsome?"

The twins may be showing signs of their age, but they hadn't lost their ability to tag-team manipulate two totally unrelated words…words as unrelated as Maddie and Parker would ever be…into a romantic relationship.

Normally, Maddie wouldn't have egged on their curiosity, but the commotion in the hall sounded like Freda was directing an entire kindergarten class to the adjoining exam room. The more time Maddie gave these dear old women, the less time she'd have for facing anymore kids today. "I think he's both," Maddie enticed.

The twins brightened with the exact same smile at the exact same moment.

"Will Parker be going back to Guatemala?" Nola Gay pushed up her glasses, her cloudy eyes huge in the thick lens. "Or is he staying around so his family can help him raise that precious little girl?"

Etta May rubbed her rough palms together. "Or maybe he'll stay around so you two can pick up where you left off?"

Maddie's conscience kicked her in the gut. The fun had gone far enough. Neither she nor Parker needed the whole town to rally behind a futile campaign to push the two of them back together. "What Parker does is his business. Not mine."

Etta May and Nola Gay studied her carefully. Etta May sadly turned her attention to her feet, but Nola Gay's keen nose for news had caught a whiff of vulnerability. Her gaze remained as sharp as a nail looking for a stud into which to hammer her suspicions. "That little Isabella is precious, isn't she?"

Maddie glanced down at the curdled milk stain covering her name and remembered how easily Isabella had warmed up to her, especially compared to the response she received from other children. "She is."

"No one's really told us exactly why Parker became this little one's legal guardian. All we know is that the poor thing's an orphan and that he did the right thing and took her in." Etta May wiped her eyes.

"Parker's going to make a wonderful father," Nola Gay said.

"He will." To that Maddie could safely agree.

"When can we visit him?" Etta May abandoned her attempt to tug up the knee-hi pantyhose that had fallen around her ankles. "We've got a fresh batch of pickles with his name on it in this very basket." She lifted the lid of the basket. Smells reminiscent of the delicious fried chicken and potato salad these ladies always brought to the church potlucks flooded the room. "Hospital food ain't too good. So, we brought our own."

"A nickel will only go so far, and we don't believe upgrading the cafeteria is the best use of our money," Nola Gay said. "Care for a chicken leg, Dr. Harper?"

"I'm on duty." Her mouth watering, Maddie had to step back from the basket. "It's going to be a few weeks before Parker's digestive system can handle pickles and chicken, or before it's safe for you to see him." Maddie noted the crimp forming in Etta May's ankle where the knee-hi seemed to be cutting into her flesh. Forgetting she was starving, she moved closer. The skin on Etta May's fleshy leg was stretched so tight it had turned purple. Alarm bells sounded in Maddie's head. "Etta May, is your ankle always so puffy?"

"Puffy?" Etta May lifted her feet straight out in front of her and peered over glasses frames that matched her sister's. "Well, I declare. That right one does look like rotten tree stump, doesn't it?"

Maddie moved closer. "Mind if I take a look?"

"Will you send us a big bill?" Nola Gay asked expectantly.

"We *want* to pay a big bill, Maddie," Etta May added. "It's why we came."

"I'm not in charge of hospital billing either." Maddie slid the stool over to the exam table. "I'm going to poke around a little before I remove your shoe, okay?"

"Whatever you think, sweet thang. You're the doctor." Etta May seemed thrilled by the prospect of having something wrong.

Maddie sat down and gently lifted Etta May's foot to her lap. "Tell me if this hurts." She pressed her thumb into the puffiness. Etta May shook her head. "How about here?" Etta May shook her head again. "Did you fall?"

"Not that I recall."

"I'm going to remove your shoe." Maddie untied Etta May's laces. The moment she pried off the orthopedic shoe, the freed foot puffed up big as a balloon. Maddie gently peeled away the knee-hi hose. Etta May's big toe and bunion were black. "Have you been on your feet a lot lately, Miss Etta May?"

"She's mostly been sittin' in the recliner." Nola Gay crossed her arms. "Been camped out there so much she's nearly worn off a coat of paint."

"Paint?" Maddie asked.

"Oh, yes," Etta May said. "We spray paint our recliners matching blue every spring."

"That sounds…thrifty." Maddie deposited the knee-hi into the empty shoe and wheeled the stool toward Nola Gay.

"We're careful with our money, especially since we had to sell our van and give up our Uber business," Nola Gay explained.

Maddie wheeled back to Etta May and removed the other shoe. "You sold the Uber van?"

Nola Gay set her sister's shoe on top of the suitcase. "Sister just didn't feel up to raking all that shag carpet anymore."

"Your Momma and Wilma Wilkerson were the only ones who used our services anyway," Etta May justified. "But don't think us destitute. That little investment fund your daddy helped us set up is brimming with money. Do you know what happens to grandmas with money in this town?"

"No, what?"

Nola Gay leaned so close to Maddie, her face serious. "Whenever a grandma dies, the funeral is at two, the family is at the bank by three, and out of town with the money by four."

"But your only family is your brother Ray, and he's older than both of you."

"Exactly," Nola Gay snorted. "If Raymond would happen to outlive us, he doesn't want or need a dime. We've got to do something with all that money before we die. And since your brother beat us to building a new gym for the kids to use at the church," she continued, "we've decided to do whatever it takes to help Leona keep good medical care in our community." Nola Gay heaved herself up from the chair and studied her sister's ankle. "Do you think Etta May has come down with something expensive, Maddie...uh, Dr. Harper?"

Maddie shrugged and handed her Etta May's other shoe and knee-hi. "Could be several things."

A hint of concern narrowed Nola Gay's eyes. "Like?"

"Something expensive would be best." Etta May seemed almost pleased that she was the one who'd come up with an illness that could put the hospital ledgers in the black. Ruthie was right, these two generous women were treasures.

Etta May's face suddenly sobered. "I can't wiggle my toes."

Maddie tried to hide her growing concern. "I'm going to admit you, Etta May and run a few tests, okay?"

Nola Gay and Etta May, unable to hide their enthusiasm, clapped their hands at the exact same time. "Sounds expensive," they said in unison.

"Very." Maddie assured them. She knew better than to try to slide Etta May's orthopedics back on. Until she could figure out the cause of this dear woman's edema, her foot was not going back into this old, black lace-up. "Wait here while I get the orders started."

CHAPTER NINE

Leona raced around the toys scattered across her living room and lunged for the cell phone she'd left on the counter. "David?"

"Hey, Momma. Sorry I couldn't answer when you called earlier. Amy and I were finishing up with Dr. Boyer."

"How is Amy?"

"Robin says she's doing great. Sugar levels are good. Her C-section incision has healed nicely." The ding of David's keys sliding into the ignition of his minivan sounded in the background. "How are the kids?"

Leona waved her tearful grandson to come to her. "That's why I called." Jamie buried his face in her leg. She rubbed his head and could tell nothing she'd done had brought his fever down. "I know you wanted to run a few errands before you came out here for dinner, but I think the kids are sick."

"We'll head that way now."

"I think that's a good idea." Leona hung up and lifted Jamie into her arms. "How about we turn on the TV and snuggle while baby sister sleeps. Sound good?"

Jamie nodded. She arranged pillows on the couch and gave him a sippy cup with diluted 7-Up. It worried her when the grands were sick and simultaneously made her miss the days when a few cartoons and some soda could make everything better for the ones she loved…especially Maddie. She and her daughter had always had a sticky relationship, but she felt the divide had grown uncrossable after she married Saul. She'd been praying about how to bridge the gap but, so far, the Lord had remained silent.

Saul emerged from his small home office and wrapped an arm around her waist. "Anything I can do?"

"Pray we don't catch whatever it is these babies have."

He kissed her temple and adjusted the sound on the blaring TV. "This doesn't have to change our plans for the evening. It'll be nice to have Maddie to ourselves."

"She'll bail on dinner if she thinks David won't be here to run interference."

"I don't think she's avoiding you."

"I haven't gotten to talk to her since she came back from Central America."

"She's been a little busy."

"I know, but—"

Saul handed Jamie the remote and led Leona to the kitchen. "I know you're disappointed that Maddie wants to stay at the parsonage, but that keeps her near the hospital. That makes it easier for her, and better for Parker." He lifted her chin. "The parsonage will probably always feel like home to her."

Of course, the parsonage was home…or what home used to be. Since J.D. died, everything had changed…her identity as a pastor's wife, her reinstatement into the working world, her financial status, the parsonage where she'd raised her family, learning to love a different man…everything but her love for her children.

"It's ironic," Leona said wistfully. "Maddie hated growing up in the glass house and now it's where she's chosen to hole up and I don't know why." Suppressed tears stung her nose. "There's time to sort things out with her, right?"

"None of us really know how much time we have." Saul had buried his first wife. He understood how important it was to set things right with loved ones. "Let her know how much you love her."

"Nothing would make me happier, but I don't know how."

"Sounds like you've got some more prayin' to do, my love." He gave her a squeeze then slipped quietly out the back door. A few minutes later, she heard his boat motor away from the dock. She wasn't the only one feeling the need for a word from the Lord.

Twenty minutes later, David and Amy pulled into the drive. Jamie's temperature had risen a full degree, and Libby had awoken from her nap crying and hotter than when Leona put her to bed.

"Sorry to miss dinner, Momma." David said as he helped Amy gather their things.

"We hate to do this to you at the last minute. We know how you were looking forward to a family dinner night." Amy jostled Libby in an effort to soothe her. "I just don't think it's a good idea to expose Maddie to a virus she could possibly carry back to Parker."

"I agree." Leona tried not to let her eyes cut to the perfectly glazed crème brûlée ramekins sitting on the counter.

"Hey, I've got an idea," David said, following her gaze. "Why don't you ask Dr. Boyer to dinner?"

"Dr. Boyer?"

"You're always saying how you and Saul want to get to know him on a personal level."

"We would love entertaining Robin, but tonight we just wanted to visit with you kids."

"Robin was just telling me how impressed he is with Maddie. She must not have cut him off at the knees because he really enjoyed having dinner with her the other night. So—"

Leona held up her palm. "Stop right there. Nothing raises Maddie's hackles faster than being forced into a situation that's not her idea. You saw how prickly she was about the welcome home party. I shouldn't have done it. Not without asking her."

"You wanted to show off your accomplished daughter. There's no crime in that, Momma—"

"She's only here for a few weeks. I'm not going to put her in another awkward situation. I think Dr. Boyer's a perfectly lovely man, but Maddie's entitled to form her own opinions. She doesn't need me meddling in the affairs of her heart."

"You're a mother. Mothers meddle." David kissed her cheek. "Your meddling saved Amy's life the day Jamie was born. Meddling now could save Maddie's soul."

"Your sister has become very self-sufficient since your father died."

"Tell you what, Momma—" David never could stand to see her heartbroken and, apparently, she wasn't doing a very good job hiding her disappointment. "—I'll handle Maddie. You call Robin."

She did want to see Maddie. If her daughter didn't feel put on the spot, maybe it would work. "Promise me you won't pressure her. If she doesn't want to do it, I'll call the whole evening off. Those steaks will keep."

"Those fancy little desserts won't." David scooped Jamie into his arms. "What would you have wanted to hear from your mother when you were Maddie's age, Momma?"

"What?"

"Think about what Grandmother could have said to you that would have saved the two of you fifty years of estrangement. Say those things to Maddie."

She remembered how hard she'd tried to have a different relationship with her children than she'd had with her own mother. It had taken J.D.'s death to bring her and her mother together. It would be just like the Lord to use the heartbreak of J.D.'s death to give her insight into how to fix Maddie's heart.

Leona shook her index finger at David. "Tell me, young man, when did you get too smart for your own good?"

He laughed and cuddle his boy close. "Maddie loves you, Momma. She's just all tangled up in grief. She's got to figure out who she's going to be now that she's no longer Daddy's little princess." He took her hand. "This is your chance to show her how wonderful it is to be Momma's girl."

CHAPTER TEN

Maddie had run out of excuses. The only way to put an end to David's high-pressure tactics was to show up for a family dinner at Momma's new lake house. She'd agreed to be pleasant not prompt.

Leaving the hospital as late as possible, she trudged toward her car. Hopefully, by the time she made her appearance everyone would be ready to eat. She could slide into her new place at Momma's new table, make small talk with her new father, eat, and then scoot out. She'd purposely not changed out of her scrubs. If Momma pushed her too hard, she'd claim the need to check on Etta May and Parker.

Maddie slowed near the turn-off road leading to the lake. To prevent dings on her fancy car and to delay her arrival further, she eased onto the gravel and proceeded at a crawl. She hadn't been to the lake since the night of Momma's wedding. Like a child, she'd turned down Momma's invitation to use their guest room and announced that if David and Amy weren't using her old room in the parsonage, she'd rather stay close to the hospital. Having easy access to Parker would aid his progress. Adding an extra layer of protection, she'd told Momma she was really looking forward to getting to know her niece and nephew.

She'd felt a twinge of guilt at Momma's disappointment, but not enough to move in with Momma and her new husband for a few weeks. It wasn't that she didn't believe her mother had the right to remarry. She did. She'd even encouraged her mother to marry Saul. So why the anger whenever she saw her mother smiling and happy again? It made no sense.

Gravel crunched beneath the Porsche's tires as she crept down Saul's driveway. Coppery rays of the setting sun danced on the water and drenched the huge trees in a fiery glow. This lush oasis was such a contrast to the dry prairies and scrub sage she'd passed on her way out of town. Such beauty was as out of place in West Texas as she.

The house, a historical limestone cottage, had been carefully restored and meticulously landscaped. Nothing about it said excessive money but compared to the leaky-roofed parsonage of Maddie's memories, Momma's new home appeared flush with cash.

Maddie took a deep breath and dragged herself out of the car. A barking, hundred-pound ball of fur bounded down the porch steps and planted two, big hairy paws on her chest. "Momma!" Maddie yelled as the beast licked her face. "Is this your dog?"

"Romeo!" Momma came running out onto the porch, a glass of tea in one hand and snapping fingers on the other. "Romeo," she snapped extra hard. "Come." She pointed to the empty spot at her feet. "Now." Both Romeo and Maddie recognized Momma's authoritative tone that spawned complete and immediate obedience.

The dog whirled and complied in one easy bound. Maddie, on the other hand, stood stock-still, determined to stave off the return of the imposed behaviors she'd fought long and hard to overcome.

Momma reached down and grabbed Romeo's collar. "I can't seem to break him of exuberant greetings." She held out the tea with a welcoming smile. "He's testing tomorrow. We're all a little nervous."

"Testing?" Maddie wiped her cheeks with her sleeve. "For what?"

"Certification."

"You don't need a test to certify that he's one huge dog."

Momma chuckled. "He's gotten a little bigger than I anticipated that's for sure." Momma glowed. "Romeo's trainer believes he has what it takes to be a medical therapy dog."

Maddie took a surprised step forward. This slobbering, energetic mutt was so different than the pedigreed cocker Momma had spoiled to an early grave. "Really?"

"Working him at the hospital will give me a way to minister to others."

And a way to spy on me. Maddie stuttered, "Soon?"

"As soon as he's certified, and I've convinced Dr. Boyer to start an animal assisted therapy program."

"I'm hoping Romeo gives her something else to housebreak besides me." Saul had joined Momma on the porch, his eyes sparkling with admiration for the woman he slid his arm around.

"I've given up on training you, Saul Levy." Momma giggled and elbowed him playfully. "Someone has to keep an eye on our investment."

Maddie's throat tightened. "Which investment?"

"Mt. Hope Memorial, of course," Momma explained. "Saul and I are doing everything we can to keep the local hospital doors open, including hiring brilliant young doctors like you and Dr. Boyer."

"Momma, I'm only here temporarily, remember?"

"That sad fact doesn't negate your brilliance." With that small quip, Maddie knew new Mrs. Levy may have changed her last name but not her old Leona-Harper-ways. Momma never really gave up. "Want to wet your whistle before our guest arrives?" An untrained ear might have missed the suspiciously upbeat tone in Momma's voice.

Gaze darting about for an ambush similar to the one she'd experienced the first night of her homecoming, Maddie took the drink. "Since when are David and Amy guests?"

Momma's hand dropped to her side. Her face went white. "Didn't your brother call you?"

"I don't think so, but I haven't had two seconds all day to check my messages."

"The kids came down with a fever this afternoon. In case it's a virus, they didn't want to expose you and risk having it carried back to Parker."

"David's not coming?"

"No."

She was not in the mood for surprises. "Bummer, and after you've gone to so much trouble and everything."

"Exactly." Momma motioned for Maddie to come sit in one of the empty chairs on the porch. "Since I'd already prepared so much food, I invited Dr. Boyer."

"You did what?"

"I've been meaning to invite him since he arrived in Mt. Hope, but it's just been one thing after another. Now that the two of you are working together, I thought—"

Maddie interrupted her mother's justifications. "I thought this was family night. You. Me. David. Amy. And the kids." From the corner of her eye, Maddie noticed Saul's mustache twitch. She immediately regretted her tone as well as her blatant exclusion of her mother's husband from the list of family members.

"Amy said she'll bring the kids out when they're feeling better, and we can try family dinner night again before—"

She didn't know what made her angrier, the thought of how close Momma and Amy were obviously becoming or that everyone had once again planned her life. "Just once, I wish you would ask me *before* launching me into one of your schemes—"

"How do you like your steak, Maddie?" Saul's attempt to change the subject was eerily similar to the way her father used to field the oil and water dust-ups between her and Momma.

The constant intrusion of thoughts of her father whenever she was around Saul fueled the emotional volcano within her. She was so focused on keeping it from erupting and spewing all over Momma that she couldn't even remember how she liked her meat.

"Maddie?" her mother prodded. When she didn't answer, Momma answered for her, "Medium well, right?"

"Medium well," she managed to grind out.

"I'll go ahead and put the meat on," Saul said to Momma. "You know how cranky I get when I'm hungry." He kissed her mother on the cheek then headed toward the smoking grill down by the gazebo.

Maddie could still feel the steam coming out of her ears. She wasn't proud of her insolent behavior. Saul had never been anything but kind to her, and he'd never tried to replace her father.

She cut her eyes at Momma. "Was that his subtle way of telling us to pull in our claws?"

"Possibly." A guilty smile tugged the corner of Momma's perfect red lips. "I still don't know him as well as I knew your father. Probably never will." Wispy traces of grief dangled between them like the string of a released balloon. "I'm sorry about not asking you before inviting Dr. Boyer. I thought it might be easier for you if..." she let her sentence trail off as her watery gaze traveled to the man whistling and messing with the grill.

Momma misses Daddy.

They finally agreed on something. Moving on was hard and it was nice to know she wasn't the only one having a rough time letting go of the bigger-than-life man they'd loved so much. Surprise shook Maddie to the core and loosened her stand-off position. She scrambled for a topic to lighten the tension. "I guess you could have invited Nellie."

"There's a current ban on fireworks," Momma deadpanned.

Maddie climbed the porch steps, tossed her keys on the wicker coffee table, and sunk into the cozy bentwood swing that faced the water.

She let her gaze drift to the man working hard to keep this evening from falling apart. "Saul's a good man, Momma."

"He is." Momma poured herself some tea and joined Maddie in the swing. "Two good men in one lifetime. I'm blessed."

Maddie waited for the other shoe to drop, for the little nudge that somehow that's all Momma wanted for her, but it didn't come.

They sipped in silence and watched the smoke from the grill float effortlessly across the lake. Maddie used to pray for the animosity between her and her mother to dissipate. She'd given up on praying when she realized that kind of quiet peace was impossible under the whir of Momma's helicopter blades.

Yet, here they were, sitting side by side with only the sounds of the cicadas between them for the first time since the limo ride to her father's funeral.

Maddie leaned closer to her mother and put her head on her shoulder. "This is nice."

Momma inhaled deeply and cupped her hand to Maddie's cheek. "It is."

Childhood memories of sitting by Momma in church bubbled to the surface. No matter how naughty Maddie had been, whenever she laid her head on her mother's shoulder, she could count on Momma to plant a forgiving love clasp on her cheek. Why couldn't she tell her mother how grateful she'd always been for her touch, how much it had meant, and how badly she missed it now?

The breeze rippling the lake carried the smell of roasting meat to Maddie's hungry stomach.

Saul waved at the smoke with a towel then opened the grill lid. "Won't be long," he shouted. "I think I see car lights."

"Dr. Boyer…" Momma cleared her throat. "…is a good man, don't you think?"

Silent alarms shattered the fragile truce. Momma hadn't given up on running her life. She'd just given up on Parker being the best solution to Maddie's happiness.

Maddie sat up. "Is that what this dinner's really about tonight?"

"Once you get to know him, I'm sure you'll come to admire him as much as we do. He thinks you're an excellent doctor."

Maddie stiffened. "The chief of staff should always tell his board chairman that her children are exceptional."

"Would it be so bad to get to know him?"

"I'm not like you. I don't need a man in my life to feel complete."

It was Momma's turn to stiffen, but she didn't. Her hand started to reach for Maddie but at Maddie's anticipatory flinch, she pulled back and lowered her voice, "Being loved and loving someone back is more than a win, Maddie. It's liberating."

"So is letting them go." Maddie hadn't meant for her words to slap Momma in the face, but from the sadness in her mother's eyes, they had. She hated making her mother feel helpless.

Saul turned toward the discord coming from the porch. "Everything okay?" he called.

Maddie felt guilty and embarrassed for acting like a petulant child, but if she was going to live her life her way, and on her terms, marry whom she pleased, or maybe never marry at all, she couldn't let Momma pressure her anymore. She stood.

"I'm sorry I ruined your plan, Momma." Maddie turned to the lake and cupped her hand to her mouth and shouted, "Saul, I hate to run out on a great meal, but I really should get back to the hospital."

Momma's face morphed into a scramble for a convincing argument. "But Robin's here." She pointed to the black convertible pulling alongside Maddie's Porsche. "What will I tell him?"

"Nothing." Maddie snagged her keys. "I can speak for myself, and I'll remind him that he hired me to care for patients." She bounded down the porch steps and stopped by Dr. Boyer's car.

The dog leapt to his feet and started after her.

"Stay, Romeo." Momma's frustrated order stopped the dog, the song of the cicadas, and Saul's flipping of the steaks.

But it did nothing to slow Maddie. "Robin."

A pleased smile lit his face. "Your mother told me you'd be here."

"Funny. She didn't mention you were coming until now."

His gaze cut to the porch where Momma stood with her hand firmly wrapped around poor Romeo's collar and tears gathering in her eyes. "Oh," he said quietly.

"Enjoy your dinner, Robin. Momma's always the hostess with the mostest." Maddie jumped into her car and sped away.

Once she reached the turn onto the highway, she pulled to a stop and took out her phone to call her brother to tell him what Momma had pulled. That's when she saw his message:

Hey, Sis. Kids sick. I suggested Momma invite Robin. Try to be nice.

CHAPTER ELEVEN

A light rapping at the door jerked Parker from his disappointment. From the moment Maddie learned of his commitment to Isabella, the distance between them had grown greater than when they were living on two different continents. Her retreat shouldn't have surprised him. Maddie had always believed she wasn't very good with kids. The summer they'd served together as camp counselors, a little girl refused to let Maddie bandage her knee. Ten minutes later, he'd found Maddie sobbing behind a tree, the first aid kit clutched to her chest.

He wanted to believe Maddie had overcome her fear of children. That her cold and clinical treatment of him had nothing to do with his decision to raise Isabella and everything to do with her all-important professionalism as his doctor. After all, she was his doctor now.

A doctor/patient relationship was the only legitimate claim he would ever have on the blonde who'd captured his heart when she bounced into his Sunday school class years ago.

Lying in this bed day after day, watching as Maddie ran her stethoscope over his chest or pressed her slender fingers against his abdomen, had given him plenty of opportunity to ponder every encounter they'd ever had. Including the two times they'd actually kissed. When he'd regained consciousness in that Central American hospital and saw her standing by his side, he'd secretly hoped she'd come running because he'd meant as much to her as she did to him.

But he wasn't delusional anymore.

Maddie's decision to come to his rescue didn't have a thing to do with him. Her decisions had always revolved around her goals and the best way to achieve them. Saving a dying guy from an infectious disease would look pretty impressive on the resume of a greenhorn epidemiologist.

It was time to put out the flame in his belly. Once and for all. He had a child to raise. Pining over a woman who didn't want children was a waste of *his* time and energy. He was going to need a bucketful of both if he was going to be a good father.

A tap at the door jolted Parker from his worries. "Come in."

The door opened slowly, then Leona stuck her head in. "Feeling up to a little company?"

"Hey, Mrs. H…I mean Mrs. L."

She waved off his little slip. "It's all right, Parker. Part of me will always be Mrs. Harper."

"Has the warden lifted my quarantine?"

Leona nodded. "I've been texting Maddie for a few days. She finally answered when I asked if you were able to have brief visits."

"You two have a falling out?"

She shrugged, but the sadness didn't leave her eyes. "I pushed way too hard…again." She put on a smile. "Anyways, Maddie says you can have limited visitors so—"

"Tell me you've smuggled in Isabella."

Leona smiled. "Surprise." She pushed the door open wider. His mother stood in the doorway with a big smile on her face, but it was the animated little girl riding on her hip that lassoed his heart.

"We promised Maddie we wouldn't stay long, and that we'd wash our hands real good," his mother said as she eased into his room. "This little sweetie's been asking for you non-stop."

"Paki."

Parker held out his arms. "Come to daddy, Isabella."

A snaggle-toothed grin lit his little girl's face and she leapt from his mother's arms into his. "Paki."

Isabella was an infusion of joy and strength, a shot in the arm stronger than anything Maddie had been dripping through his IV. "I can tell someone's been taking very good care of you, Sugar Bean." He smiled at his mother who was beaming at the sight of her son holding a child. "Thanks, Mom."

His mother waved off his praise. "This girl loves my biscuits and gravy."

"Everybody loves Kathy's biscuits and gravy." Leona pulled a chair over by Parker's bed and insisted that his worn-out mother sit for a moment. "I think I'll run down and check on the Story sisters. That'll give you three some time to catch up."

Once Leona was out the door, Parker's stored-up emotions spilled out. "I'm sorry Mom. I should have called, but it all happened so fast with Isabella. I intended to tell you in person. Then I got sick. I shouldn't have let Maddie bring me home."

His mother put her index finger to her lips. "Shhh. Parker, Maddie's kept you alive. You've given us a beautiful granddaughter. We're blessed. No need for apologies or second guessing." She patted his arm. "Your dad wanted me to tell you that he would have come today but there wasn't room for a wheelchair and a car seat in your truck."

"How's his hip?" Parker stayed Isabella's fingers poking the buttons on his bed control. She snatched up the TV remote and pointed it at the screen on the wall.

"He should be kicking up dust and getting in my hair again in a couple of weeks." True to form, his mother saw good in every situation, including an unexpected grandchild. "He's able to wheel out to the fence and check on the livestock." She inclined her head toward Isabella who was whacking the remote on his bed rail and whispered, "This one is as busy as a raccoon in a campground. The garden would have suffered had it not been for Nellie."

"Nellie?"

His mom reached for Isabella's little fingers and smiled when the little girl dropped the remote and grabbed hold. "Nellie said, Kathy I'll make sure the tomatoes don't rot. You make sure Isabella is happy. Grandbabies don't stay small forever." His mom paused, chewing on the corner of her lip as she mulled something over in her mind. "Nellie's turned down right...thoughtful."

Parker's face scrunched in disbelief. "You don't say?"

"You would hardly recognize her."

"Does Isabella like Nellie?"

"Not really," Parker's mother said with her kindest and most hopeful smile. "But Isabella hasn't really taken up with anyone other than me and Maddie."

"Maddie?"

"I could hardly pry her loose from Maddie when they got off that fancy jet Leona rented."

"Are we talking about the same girl? Because the Maddie Harper I know hates kids and anyone who doesn't."

His mother sighed. "I was hopin' you'd gotten shed of her in the jungle."

He let out a resigned sigh. "Me too."

"Maddie doesn't hate kids, and she certainly doesn't hate you."

"Maybe not, but most kids don't like her."

"Well, Isabella's taken with her." His mother caught the confusion in his eyes and hurried on. "I'm sure if we give Nellie time, she'll win this little cutie over, too. Nellie's crazy about Isabella. Always bringing her some little treat or a cute little outfit." His mom sat back and took in the scene of Isabella climbing all over him. "We're not the only ones who've grown very attached."

Parker pulled his daughter away from his IV line and drew her close, inhaling the scent of baby shampoo and sausage gravy. "She's pretty much got me whipped."

"You always did like headstrong women." His mother loved Maddie, too, and he could see she'd dreamed of them being together for as long as he had, but wisely she changed the subject. "I know you've probably not had the strength to make a new life plan, but please tell me you're not in a hurry to take Isabella back to Guatemala."

"Mom." Parker rubbed his thumb over Isabella's soft hand, stalling for a way to let his mother down easy. "I didn't have the chance to finish installing the water system my village desperately needs. That's why typhoid hit us so hard. Without access to fresh water, we're fighting a losing battle."

"*Your* village?"

"They're like family."

"But *this* child needs a real family. A home. An education. Grandparents. A mother."

"I'll figure it out."

"You know your father and I want to spoil her rotten, right?"

"From the look on your face, I'd have a hard time trying to stop you."

"Then don't."

Someone knocked on the door. Before Parker could answer, Nellie waltzed in. Two big shopping bags hung from her arms. She'd turned thoughtful all right…every detail of her appearance had been well-calculated. Green eyes sparkling with concern. Auburn hair piled just high enough to expose her tan shoulders and toned arms.

A black tank top clung to her perfect form. Tight, white shorts set off those long legs bronzed from the hours she'd spent helping his parents take care of his ranch.

Nellie was stunning. Gratitude for her *thoughtful* assistance during his recovery was not the response stirring under his hospital gown.

"A Hallmark moment if I ever saw one." Nellie beamed her beautiful white smile at Parker. "Don't let me interrupt."

"Of course you're not interrupting, is she, Parker?" His mom waved Nellie closer.

He shifted Isabella away from her second attempt to remove his IV from his hand. "We were just reconnecting."

Nellie's attention skipped over Isabella and glided the length of Parker's body. "You're looking far better than Maddie let on." Her attention lingered at his mid-section longer than he was comfortable with. "I came by earlier, but Maddie wouldn't even let me poke my head in."

"She's following contagious-disease protocol." Parker tugged the sheet over an exposed leg, all the while giving himself a mental kick for jumping to Maddie's defense. His doctor had made it abundantly clear she could take care of herself. Time he did the same.

Nellie let her gaze slowly travel back to Parker's face. "If I was *Dr.* Harper, I'd want to keep all the handsome patients to myself, too." How did she do that purr-thing between her clenched-teeth smile? "We're all so glad you're home."

Isabella's little hands patted his face, snapping Parker from the trance of Nellie's swaying hips and persimmon-colored lips. "Thanks for lending my folks a hand, Nellie."

"Oh. My. Goodness." She set the sacks on the foot of his bed and leaned in and tickled Isabella under the chin. "Who could stay away from this angel?"

Isabella let out a big wail, turned her back to Nellie, then buried her face in Parker's chest.

Undaunted by the rejection, Nellie reached into one of the shopping bags. "I promised you a little surprise, Bella." She pulled out an open-faced box holding a cloth doll with dark yarn hair. "I ordered this baby because she looks like you."

Parker stroked his daughter's head, not sure he liked Nellie feeling free to spoil his daughter or hang a nickname around her neck without his permission. But this child had lost so much. A little extra female attention would probably do her good. "Look, *Isabella*." He emphasized his child's full name and gently pried her grip from his gown. "Nellie brought you a doll."

"She has a baby bottle." Nellie kept pulling things out of the sack. "And a little diaper bag. And look at this." She dragged out a small pink cradle. "A little bed for your baby."

Isabella was not easily bought. She clung to him and gave Nellie the fisheye. But when Nellie pulled out a soft pink blanket to wrap the baby in, Isabella began to ease from his lap. Parker couldn't help but make a note at how useful the promise of comfort was when it came to instilling courage. He had to admit, this kinder, gentler Nellie was far different than the hellcat that had once cornered David Harper in the baptistry changing room and left braces' marks on his neck.

He gave a grateful nod and said, "Thanks, Nellie."

She waved off his gratitude with a quick flick of her long finger to her lip. "Shhh."

He watched as Isabella inched toward the toy bounty and snatched the doll. "Baby?" She handed the box to Parker, indicating he should free her prize from the twist ties holding it to the cardboard backing.

"Yay!" Nellie clapped her hands and glowed at Parker. "Every girl needs a baby to love." All those years in braces had been worth it because Nellie's smile was a dazzler. Before he knew it, Parker felt himself smiling right back at her.

A small knock and then Leona poked her head in again. "Look who I found wandering the halls and saving the world." She pushed the door open and dragged Maddie into the room by the arm of her white coat. From Maddie's expression she and her mother had not made up and coming to his room at Leona's bidding was not Maddie's idea. But she was holding a small plate wrapped in cellophane in one hand and a piece of paper in the other.

"Maa-d!" Isabella threw her new doll to the floor and scrambled out of Parker's grasp. She flung her chubby little arms around Maddie's neck and wrapped her legs around Maddie's waist.

Maddie's eyes were two huge dinner plates, but her arms whipped around and secured the little girl in a flash, all without dropping the pie or paper still in her hands.

"Well, I declare," Parker's mom elbowed Leona.

"Well, isn't that…something?" Leona stuttered.

"Well, I never." Nellie huffed.

"Momma!" Isabella buried her face in Maddie's white coat.

His mother jumped up from her chair. "Maddie!" She hugged Maddie, sandwiching Isabella between them. "Thank you for saving my boy." She put a hand on Isabella's head. "And for bringing me the greatest gift of all…my grandbaby."

Color flushed Maddie's cheeks. "Happy to help."

"We all want to know when Parker can go home," Nellie purred.

Maddie's eyes darted toward him. He felt that familiar urge to help her out of this awkward corner. But he didn't. She wanted to go it alone. The time had come to let her.

"These are your latest labs." Maddie offered him the paper in her usual show of strength then backed away from his bed with Isabella still clinging to her neck. "Your blood cultures are clear. I can sign your release as soon as the nurses get it ready."

Delighted squeals, followed by hugs exchanged between Leona, his mother, and Nellie, sent Isabella scrambling to get even closer to Maddie.

Over the hubbub, Parker noticed Maddie didn't seem to mind Isabella's vice-like grip. His two favorite girls were locked in their own world. Isabella staring at Maddie. Maddie smiling at his daughter and stroking her hair. Maddie could be hard-headed, distant, and super self-reliant. But she was still Maddie. The girl who'd always been in his corner. The girl who'd risked hurting him again to save him.

He was the one pouting like an ungrateful and wounded schoolboy. Withholding his friendship. Withholding the truth about how he felt. Generally acting the fool. Had he really stooped so low?

He heard Isabella giggle and looked at Maddie again. She was staring at him with a mixture of pleasure and angst on her face. If he didn't know better, he could have sworn she was blinking back tears.

He stomped the dormant possibilities springing up within him like watered seeds. "Thanks for getting me out of here alive."

She swallowed hard and continued from a safe distance, "You'll have to have your stool cultured several times over the next three months to make sure haven't relapsed or that you're not a typhoid carrier. Dr. Boyer has agreed to monitor your progress."

"Dr. Boyer?" The disappointment he thought he'd disguised so well landed with a thud in his raw belly. "I thought *you* were my doctor."

Everyone quieted. All eyes turned to Maddie. Sweat beads popped out on her forehead.

"I'm only here for a couple more weeks."

Isabella took Maddie's face between her hands. "Momma?"

Parker tried to hide the blow Maddie's leaving would be to his daughter's heart, and his own, by switching gears. "Is that pie for me?"

Maddie flushed again. "It is," she said with a forced-looking smile. "To celebrate."

"I hope its pecan."

If she'd caught his reference to the night they'd spent in a blizzard and the kiss he could still taste, she didn't let it show on her face. "No nuts for you yet, mister. Still need to go easy on your digestive track." She stepped forward, holding the pie out to him. "It's buttermilk chess. Bette Bob brought some by for Etta May and when I told her how much you like pie, she insisted on sharing."

He set the pie on his tray. "Thanks again, Maddie. I owe you one."

"I owed you...for the wrecked pickup, remember?"

She had caught his reference. Did she think about that kiss? Pleasure rippled through him. He motioned for Isabella. "Come to Paki."

His daughter shook her head and said, "I want Maa-d."

CHAPTER TWELVE

"Don't make a mountain out of a mole hill, Momma." Maddie strode through the hospital corridors, her mother hot on her trail. "She recognized me. That's all."

"But Isabella has flat-out refused to have a thing to do with me, Nellie, or even Parker's father. The only people she'll go to is Parker, Kathy, and…you. Had he told you about her?"

Maddie ground to a stop outside Etta May's slightly ajar door. "I didn't know Parker had a kid until his landlord thrust her into my arms exactly two minutes before our plane took off. The poor thing had obviously never flown. She was a frightened little bunny willing to crawl into a wolf's lap if it would keep her from falling from the sky."

"You and animals have always gotten along fine. But you and kids…well…"

Maddie whirled, fire on her tongue. "Enough."

Hurt, understanding, and a horrifying realization that she'd once again pushed too hard swept across Momma's face and froze her still beautiful features in shocked disbelief. "I'm sorry, sweetheart. For everything. Especially the other night."

"No, I'm the one who should apologize." Maddie swallowed her pride. "Once I got phone service, David's message came through. Why didn't you tell me the whole Dr. Boyer thing was his idea?"

"Would it have made a difference?"

"Yes…no…I don't know." Maddie reached for the handle of Etta May's door. "I've got patients to see."

"Maddie." Momma grabbed her hand. "I shouldn't have implied you needed a man to make you happy. And I shouldn't have invited Dr. Boyer without your permission. It's your life. Live it your way." She leaned in and kissed Maddie's cheek. "Don't ever let anyone tell you what will make you happy. Not even me."

These words were the very words Maddie had been longing to hear for years. She'd fought long and hard to shatter the glass cage Momma and the folks in this small town had dropped over the preacher's daughter. "I'm sorry I'm such a disappointment."

"Disappointment? Madison Harper why in the world would you think you're a disappointment?"

"I'm not David…and I'm not you."

"Me?"

"I'm never going to marry, have two kids, move back to Mt. Hope and sit in church every Sunday."

"Is that what you think I want for you? My life? My choices?"

"Yes."

"Baby, I love my life. But the only part of it I'd wish on you is the happiness I've had…still have. I've always wanted you to be happy. That's why I've been so protective. I thought if I could make your life perfect, you wouldn't have to suffer."

"But I have suffered. Daddy died." Maddie couldn't believe she'd just said that. Momma had not pushed her father into the pulpit and ordered him to have a heart attack. "I'm sorry, Mom—" But her apology came too late. Momma was scurrying for the exit.

Telling her mother how she really felt was supposed to make her feel better. Instead, her heart ached. Maddie swiped at the tears burning her cheeks, took a deep breath, and blew out slowly. She was nearly thirty years old. A highly educated medical professional more than capable of taking care of herself. Time to quit acting like a spoiled baby and start acting like a decent adult.

She knocked lightly on Etta May's door.

"Door's open." Nola Gay had added an impressive collection of doilies and crocheted afghans to the stark décor of the hospital room. Sunlight streamed through the jars of pickles lined up neatly along the windowsill.

Nola Gay followed the trajectory of Maddie's bouncing gaze and nodded toward the pickles. "I hope you don't mind if we pass them out to the fine nurses and doctors as a little thank you for their kind attention."

"I'm sure they'll be grateful." Maddie eased toward Etta May's bed, her eyes taking in the old woman's pale coloring. "Most patients never say thank you."

Etta May reached up and took her hand. "You, okay?" Etta May's dentures were soaking in a glass on her bedside table, so her lips caved in around her bare gums, making her speech difficult to understand.

"I'm good. How are you?"

"I'm dying until my bill reaches fifty thousand, remember?" Etta May winked.

Maddie lifted the sheet to check on Etta May's swelling. "Where are your compression socks?"

"I took 'em off so Nola Gay could rinse them out." Etta May pointed to the socks dripping from the extended arm of the TV swivel-mount.

"You've got to keep them on."

"But they're so uncomfortable," Etta May argued.

Nola Gay came to Etta May's rescue and said, "Word on the prayer chain is that Parker could be dismissed from the hospital."

That blasted prayer chain was a noose around her neck. "Is that so?"

"I knew it!" Nola Gay's eyes twinkled. "You *have* dismissed him, haven't you?"

Maddie let out a heavy sigh. "Yes."

"Praise the Lord!" the twins whispered in unison.

"I'll confirm the rumor and activate the prayer chain's shouts of praise," Nola Gay dug for her phone.

Maddie turned to her patient whose permed curls and uneven bangs matched the pillows stuffed around her head. "Wouldn't expect any less."

"Parker loves our pickles," Etta May whispered.

Maddie had always thought of the twins as eternal, like the never-ending west Texas winds that bent the spindly mesquites and constantly rearranged her hair. Now, with Etta May's numbers showing an irregular heartbeat and Nola Gay's clothes hanging from her skeletal frame, she realized she wasn't prepared to lose another person she loved. Momma would be well within her rights to never speak to her again.

"Would you mind dropping off a couple of jars at his ranch when you go to see that he's settled?" Nola Gay asked.

"I wasn't planning to make a house call—"

"A little welcome home gift from us would mean so much to him," Etta May pressed.

"I won't be…" Maddie stopped, not wanting to explain her reluctance to see Parker again. "Sure. Pick out the ones you want me to take."

Nola Gay lowered the footrest on her recliner and heaved herself up to the window ledge. "Sister, did Parker like the sweets or the dills?"

"He said the candied spears reminded him of us." Etta May flashed a gummy smile. "Sweet and spicy."

"Candied it is, then." Nola Gay selected two jars filled with ruby red spears floating in a tangy liquid of sugar and vinegar. "Give him our love, too." She carefully deposited the jars in Maddie's arms. "Tell him to bring that precious baby girl of his up to see us once he gets her all squared away."

"We've heard she's just beautiful," Etta May said. "Busy as a one-armed bandit, but precious."

"She's very cute," Maddie admitted.

"Kathy says she's real picky about who she takes up with." Nola Gay's raised brows and expectant stare implied more than a statement. She was probing for extra prayer-chain fodder.

Maddie noticed the untouched dinner tray she'd had the kitchen double and jumped on the chance to change the subject. "Don't either of you feel like eating?"

Etta May wrinkled her nose. "This hospital okra could slime the Brazos."

"Boiled greens give us the trots," Nola Gay agreed, "and Sister's just not up to popping in and out of bed."

Maddie worried about their matching loss of appetites. "What *does* sound good?" She'd heard of sympathy pains, but maybe Momma was right. One twin goes, the other wouldn't be far behind. "You both need to keep up your strength."

Etta May rubbed her stomach. "I've been cravin' your momma's chicken pot pie."

"Leona's pot pie is easy on the bowels." Nola Gay rubbed her stomach. "Your daddy used to say there was nothin' like one of Leona's pot pies to fix what ails you."

Maddie's gaze darted between Etta May and Nola Gay. They'd overheard the argument she'd had with her mother and were setting up a reason for her and Momma to patch things up. "I'll text her and let her know. I'm sure Momma will be happy to do whatever she can to shorten your stay."

"Then not a word to Leona, do you hear?" Etta May's eyes narrowed. "We don't want our stay shortened."

"You're not going anywhere until I'm convinced those blood thinners and clot busters I have you on are working. If they don't, we'll have to talk about surgery."

Etta May's eyes widened in horror. "Surgery?" She turned to Nola Gay. "Can't we just write them a check, Sister? I don't want to be cut on."

"We'd just need to insert a little filter into a vein in your abdomen."

Etta May shook her head. "Please, Maddie. No surgery."

Maddie sighed. "Okay. Not right now. But you've got to promise me you'll wear those compression socks and start eating."

"She's right, Sister. We'll need our strength if we're going to keep the hospital meter running." Nola Gay stacked another jar of pickles on Maddie's load. "Your momma's new husband loves our candied spears. Sweetness always goes over so good with the men folk." She eased back into the recliner. "You can leave these with him. Their place is on the way to Parker's."

"I know where Momma lives."

"Then why don't you go see her?"

She'd thrown Momma over the cliff and these old foxes were willing to bulldoze her over if she didn't at least try to repair the horrible mess she'd made of her most treasured relationships. "Okay, I'll go. But it may take me a day or two to get out there. I'm pretty swamped."

Satisfied smiles stretched the wrinkles from both the old girls' faces.

"You're the one whose biological clock is ticking." Nola Gay cranked the recliner handle and her legs shot out in front of her. "Not us."

CHAPTER THIRTEEN

It was almost dark by the time Maddie left the clinic. Cicadas thrummed in the branches of the mesquite trees that dotted the parking lot. She'd not had a moment to sit since sunrise. No wonder she was numb with exhaustion. Juggling three pickle jars, she was so engrossed in trying to click her key fob without dropping the jars that she didn't dare turn to identify the car that had pulled up beside her.

"I was going to ask if you were hungry, but I see the Storys beat me to it." Dr. Boyer had the top down on his convertible and an easy smile on his face.

"I hate pickles." Maddie steadied the pickles with her chin and opened the passenger door to her car. She carefully set the jars on the seat.

"How about joining me for a steak?"

He was flirting. Outright, bold coming on to her. "At the Koffee Kup?"

He gave a brief shake of his head. "For the sake of our arteries, maybe we should avoid Ruthie's."

"You didn't have any trouble choking down that burger."

"Ruthie's burgers are surprisingly good. And her steaks are fair when I'm in a hurry. But tonight, I feel like savoring a slab of well-aged prime beef."

"Sounds expensive." Maddie glanced down at the body fluids splattered on her scrubs not fifteen minutes ago by a kid who'd eaten a grasshopper. "I look awful."

"I'm still in my scrubs. I've already reserved my table. It's hidden away in a dark corner of the deck. No one will see us."

"It's been a long week." She started around the back of her car. "I'm headed to the shower, and then plan to sleep the entire weekend."

"Make me eat alone and I'll tell the board you signed on for *two* months of family clinic work." He revved his engine. "Come on. I'll race you. Loser buys."

The cocky challenge raised her chin. "And the winner gets what?"

His appraising look didn't seem the least bit put off by the weariness on her face. "Winner gets a day's reprieve from family clinic duty."

A day without kids was a no-brainer. "Deal."

She ran around and jumped into her car. Before she could press the ignition button, the squeal of rubber told her Boyer's convertible had left the parking lot.

"Jerk."

Maddie's hair whipped from the band holding it in place as her Porsche flew over the deserted highway. She inhaled deeply. The earthy scent of a possible thunderstorm swirled in the wind. She had no business having dinner with the chief of staff. Again. But the prospect of talking to an adult after a day of traumatizing encounters with sick kids had its appeal. Spending so many hours at the hospital since she'd taken on Parker and the clinic had taught her something important. If she was going to be happy, the way Momma wanted her to be happy, maybe she needed more in her life than her work. Once settled into her new job in Atlanta, she'd take time to make friends…maybe even open herself up to a romantic relationship. Having a private life should be so much easier in a city too large for everyone to make it their business to know her business.

In no hurry to end this budding sense of direction, she eased off the gas. Dr. Boyer deserved a win. Not because of all he'd done to grant her temporary hospital privileges, but because he'd stayed out of her way. At the very least, she owed him a steak and possibly even a couple of extra days at the clinic.

Ten miles south of town, Maddie followed the convertible's taillights into a gravel parking lot. Multi-colored Christmas lights lit the huge wraparound porch of the rustic, log-cabin style steakhouse.

Though it was dark, the temperature hovered around ninety.

Dr. Boyer opened the restaurant's heavy wooden door and said, "Ladies first." His poor attempt to mimic a southern drawl brought a smile to Maddie's face.

Inside, the air conditioner blasted while a fire burned in the big stone hearth. A huge metal sign hung over the hostess station. It promised a free meal to anyone brave enough to consume their famous 72-ounce steak in one hour.

"We'll sit on the deck." Robin winked at the cute little hostess eyeing him admiringly.

Recognition lit her eyes. "Follow me, Dr. Boyer." Hips swaggering seductively, the girl led them through huge double doors. Maddie wasn't surprised when the hostess slipped him a napkin with her number scribbled on it, or when Robin slid it into the chest pocket of his scrub shirt with a flirty pop to his heart.

What Maddie didn't expect was the tremendous view from the expansive, tin-covered deck that had been built atop thick cedar pilings driven deep into the water. Pink bougainvillea spilled out of old whiskey barrels and rusty wagon wheels formed the railing that linked to hand-hewn porch posts. Bleached longhorn skulls nailed to the outside wall of the restaurant lent their horns as hat racks for the rugged men with red faces and rancher tans sitting at tables with their tired wives and rowdy kids.

"Wow!" Maddie said as the hostess seated them in a cozy table far from the noise of the live band and patrons nursing cold beers. "Nothing screams fun like a night out with the kids."

Dr. Boyer nodded to a striking woman serving the ranchers sweet tea. "That's the owner's wife. She was a high-risk patient I delivered successfully. I always reward risky ventures with my patronage."

"Patronage?" Maddie dropped into her chair, an unexpected wave of admiration and exhaustion suddenly getting the better of her. "Do you always sound so stuffy?"

"Only when I'm nervous."

She scoffed. "I don't think anything makes you nervous."

"That's an uncharacteristically wrong diagnosis, Dr. Harper. Beautiful women make me shake in my shoes."

"You weren't shaking when that perky little waitress slipped you her number."

His eyes locked with Maddie's. "There's a difference between attractive and stunning."

"Then you picked a strange profession because I'm pretty certain unattractive women aren't the only ones who suffer pregnancy complications."

"Are you always as subtle as a defibrillator?"

"Are you always on the prowl?"

"Like you, I haven't found a compelling reason to settle down."

Had she given up her dreams and stayed in Mt. Hope, she'd probably be married to Parker, have a couple of rowdy children of her own, and have wrinkles that made her look old before her time.

Steering the conversation away from the dangerously personal territory, Maddie lifted the large leather menu. "Order up, Chief. I'm buying."

"I can pay my own way."

"A bet's a bet. I lost the race. Besides, I'm rich, remember?"

"So am I." He smirked at her lack of surprise. His long, slender fingers formed two arrows he pointed at himself. "Indulged only child of a busy surgeon and detached mother." Then, tossing the ball in her court, he pointed the fingered arrow at her.

"Stifled daughter of a small-town pastor and the woman for whom the term 'helicopter mom' was coined."

"Leona seems lovely."

"She is. Especially when she's softening you up. You know she's softening you up, right?"

"I granted your privileges, what else could she possibly need?"

"She's acquired a rescue dog."

"And?"

"She's training him to be a medical therapy dog."

"I've seen animal-assisted therapy programs. They're great." His brows drew together. "But my hospital doesn't offer that program."

"Yet." When her point dawned on his face, she couldn't help but chuckle at his pricelessly cornered expression. "And it's not *your* hospital."

"You know what I meant."

Surgeons weren't usually so easily flustered. This was fun. "Consider yourself, Leona'd."

"Leona'd?"

"Manipulated to suit Momma's purposes." Maddie wiped the condensation forming on her water glass. "I've been Leona'd my entire life." Like being told all Momma had ever wanted was for her to be happy.

He pressed his straw through the paper wrapper. "Ah, thus the reason you're in a hurry to move across the country." And just like that, he'd lobbed the perfect grenade to fluster her.

The first time she watched her mother yield to an angry church member, Maddie made the deliberate choice to take a different path than the one her mother had chosen. She didn't want to live too scared to do anything that might offend someone and put her livelihood in jeopardy. She wanted freedom to wear what she wanted, work if she wanted, and live where she wanted. Her rebellion took many forms. She refused to learn to cook, marry a good church boy, have a house full of kids, and serve the church for free. She wanted to be happy...on her terms.

The contradiction hit her hard. Her mother was happy. She'd always been happy. Even when life was hard, her mother seemed to have some sort of irritating internal buoyancy that kept her afloat despite her fear of drowning.

Maddie shrugged. "It's a good offer."

Thick, sizzling steaks with sides of red-skinned potatoes and grilled asparagus smothered in garlic butter arrived. Robin swallowed the first delicious bite then steered the conversation to Atlanta's proximity to the east coast and all the important medical connections she could make.

His interest in her career quickly morphed into the plans he had for his own career. He'd come here to clear his conscience and his name. He'd never expected to experience the healing he'd found in Mt. Hope. Now that he'd accomplished his purpose, he intended to use his newly acquired management skills as a steppingstone into big-city hospital administration. Listening to him was like listening to...herself.

Ambition had driven her to rise above the disadvantages of being a preacher's daughter from a small, Texas high school. It had driven her to study harder for the MCAT than anyone in her pre-med classes and dared her to apply for the best med schools. She'd always been proud of her ambition. But it was a sobering, sickening thing when clawing your way to the top was the only thing two people had in common. Ambition had been the mutual attraction between her and her old boyfriend Justin, the snowboarder who went on to win Olympic gold. In the end, it was the inability to look out for anything other than their own interests that tore them apart.

Suddenly bone-weary and slightly nauseated, Maddie gathered her purse. "I have an early call at the clinic tomorrow."

Robin reached across the table and took her hand. "See me again."

She shook her head. "What's the point? I'm leaving."

"Not for two weeks." He held her fingers, seductively running his thumb over hers. A devilish smile caressed his handsome features. "It could be fun."

"I haven't had time for fun in years."

CHAPTER FOURTEEN

Saturday morning the west wind blew in hot and dusty. It whooshed through the open bedroom window and lifted the plastic drop cloth Parker had spread over the hardwood floor. He'd chosen to convert the room across from his small master suite into Isabella's nursery. If his daughter cried out in the night, he wanted her within easy reach of his comfort.

"Look out, Sugar Bean!" Isabella chased after him as he raced to set a full paint can on one corner of the plastic and his step stool on the other. "What you laughin' at, little girl?" He scooped her up and twirled her around. He got in a few kisses on the soft spot on her neck that still smelled of last night's bubble bath thanks to Nellie's gifts. "We've got work to do." He set Isabella in the middle of the cleared-out room. "Let's see if we can get more paint on the walls than on us. Okay?"

Isabella picked up a dry brush and started pounding on a paint can.

He'd let his mother and Nellie select the crib, the bedding, and the paint. Once they'd gathered everything he needed for the redecorating project, they'd helped him get settled in for his first night back at the ranch. But after Isabella's bath, he'd sent his parents back to their own spread.

Despite everyone's protests, his mom needed a rest from double-duty caregiving, his father needed to heal, and he and Isabella needed time to figure this father-daughter stuff out on their own. And Nellie? Well, he had to admit that in his weakened condition, it had been nice having an extra set of hands when it came to Isabella's care, feedings, and baths. But he could tell from the way Isabella clung to his leg that she wasn't crazy about the loud and flashy redhead.

Then again, Nellie had always been an acquired taste. One he'd never been interested in acquiring…until last night. After Isabella had finally fallen asleep, he'd invited Nellie to crash with him on the porch swing. He didn't know if the moment of stupidity had been caused by the warm night air, Nellie's perfume, or the euphoria of his meds, but the surprisingly comfortable experience had brought on thoughts of how nice it would be to have someone to share his concerns for Isabella's well-being.

Maddie's right. Raising a child alone isn't going to be easy.

He hated to admit that Maddie—the woman his daughter had taken to calling momma—was right. Even more, he hated how images of the beautiful doctor kept pushing against his efforts to silence them. This bland diet she'd put him on was beginning to pump up his strength, but his feelings still lagged. They seemed hung up on what could have been.

He turned to the sound of ripping cellophane, but he was too slow. Isabella had already stuffed the plastic from the unwrapped roller cover in her mouth.

"No, Sugar Bean." He hurried to her and dug wet plastic out of her mouth. He snagged the new roller cover and squatted beside her. "Play with this." He handed her the fuzzy tube.

She rubbed it over his face and across his hair. They both started giggling. Pleased he'd found something to keep her entertained, he stood. "Okay, let's get back to work."

She threw the roller cover across the room, grabbed a screwdriver, and ran.

"No, Sugar Bean. That's too sharp." He chased her down and pried it from her fingers.

Isabella threw herself on the floor and started crying.

He was going to need more than strength of body to keep up with this tiny wrecking ball. But he was still a few weeks away from gaining his full stamina. Just setting up to paint the nursery had worn him out. How was he going to sling paint and have enough juice left in him to follow Isabella around today? Maybe he shouldn't have sent his mother home?

Dr. Boyer had recommended he stay in the States for at least a year. Allow his health to return and give his body plenty of time to recover. Make certain he was free of relapses before he submitted his immune system to the required typhoid vaccinations he'd need to go back to Central America.

His mother would be pleased. She'd made her wishes very clear. And she was right. Mt. Hope was a great place to raise a child. He'd always pictured himself chasing a dozen kids around his little ranch. A year would fly by. Probably way too fast. But it wouldn't change the fact that he'd fallen in love with the work in Guatemala.

"Want to help Paki tape?" He held up a blue roll and she quit crying.

For every piece he put down, it seemed Isabella went behind him pulling up two. A job that should have taken ten minutes ended up gobbling up an hour.

After he finally finished taping the drop cloth to the baseboards, Parker stripped Isabella down to her diaper. "Here, Sugar Bean." He gave her a small bucket of water and a clean paintbrush. "You work on those walls over there while I start painting over here."

He cranked the volume on the country and western radio station he'd missed while he was out of the country and sang louder with each swipe of his roller.

"Parker!" The familiar voice calling him over the music sounded irritated.

He wheeled, paint dripping from his brush. "Maddie?"

Isabella dropped her paint brush in the water bucket and charged toward the door. "Maa-d!" She hit Maddie's knee-caps full force and flung her arms around Maddie's legs. "Maa-d!"

Holding a jar of pickles in each hand, Maddie swayed to maintain her balance. "Look out, sweet girl."

"Isabella!" Parker dropped his roller in the tray. His first step landed in his daughter's water bucket. His arms flew up in search of something to stop his fall, but gravity won. He crashed face-first into the open, half-empty bucket of paint, slid five feet, then landed in a sprawl.

"Parker!" Maddie managed to set the pickles down, scoop up Isabella, and fly to his side. "Are you alright?"

Princess Pink dripped from his nose.

Maddie wiped a drip from his chin. "Pink's not really your color." The giggle she'd been holding back erupted. It turned into laughter she couldn't control. She laughed so hard she had to sit down beside him. Isabella remained threaded tightly around her neck. "Your Daddy has always had smooth moves," she managed to choke out to his worried, wide-eyed little girl as she handed him a roll of paper towels.

Parker pushed himself upright and mopped his face. "Wait until she sees my basketball layup."

Now they were both laughing. Isabella relaxed her hold and began to giggle but when Parker held out his arms to relieve Maddie, his daughter refused to budge. "Momma," she insisted, stubbornly burying her face into Maddie's chest.

Over the top of ebony curls, Parker's gaze united with Maddie's. Neither of them had the heart to correct Isabella's claim.

"I may not have smooth moves, but I know better than to mess with a woman who knows what she wants." Parker dragged his wet palms down the front of his old t-shirt and left two pink swaths. "I've got more paint on me than the walls."

Maddie swallowed hard and waved at what he had painted. "Looks like somebody's going to have a princess room...complete with a handsome pink prince."

He raised the edge of his t-shirt and swiped at his wet cheek. "Every girl deserves a prince."

"Not every girl needs one."

"Sucks for me." He offered Maddie his hand.

Maddie laughed and allowed him to pull her and Isabella to their feet. "Need some help knocking this out?"

He suddenly realized he hadn't let go of Maddie's hand and dropped it quickly. "I've got my trusty assistant."

Maddie tickled Isabella's bare tummy. "She's dressed for easy cleanup."

"She's lucky I'm a patient man or she'd be wearing an orange jumpsuit with an inmate number on the back." He reached over and tickled Isabella, too. "You love to keep your old man hoppin', don't you, Sugar Bean?"

"Sugar Bean?" The name sounded surprisingly comfortable rolling off Maddie's tongue. "I like it." She stroked Isabella's head. "It suits you, little one."

How could a woman stroking a child's head be so incredibly attractive? Maddie looked up and caught him staring.

Searching for something to fill the first awkward silence, he spotted the canning jars by the door. "Pickles?"

"From the Storys. I said I'd deliver them." Isabella wiggled to get down, so Maddie lowered her to the drop cloth. "But you can't have a single bite. Not while you're on a soft diet." She wagged her index finger for emphasis. "Which you *are* sticking to, right?"

He gave a little salute. "Absolutely, General Harper."

"Paki, paint." Isabella held out her empty water bucket and ordered, "Paint."

"Sorry, Sugar Bean. Daddy's made a mess of things again."

"Here, let me." Maddie took the bucket and hurried off to the bathroom to fill it with water.

Parker finished wiping paint from his face and ran his fingers through his hair. The room was a wreck. His daughter had paint all over her body. And his emotions were spinning faster than the roller he'd been pushing over the walls.

"Here you go, Sugar Bean." Maddie set the bucket in front of Isabella and handed her the clean paint brush.

Isabella tugged Maddie's hand. "Paint, peez."

Maddie shot Parker a look he couldn't quite decipher. Knowing Maddie and her aversion to kids, he opted to take the help-me-out course.

"Really, Maddie, you don't have to stay. I'm sure you've got places to go and people to save."

She took the brush Isabella offered. "If we all work together, we can knock this out in an hour."

"But you'll get paint on those fancy jeans."

"Not if you've got an old t-shirt I can borrow."

His breath caught in his throat when she stepped out of the bathroom with her hair pulled up and wearing his faded Texas A&M shirt. She'd always seemed bigger than life, but the sleeves came past her elbows and the hem covered her knees. How could so much strength be crammed into such a perfect little body?

"All right, then." She picked up a roller and flashed a determined smile. "Let's do this."

It was hard to concentrate with the sweet scent of her so close, but three hours later and two more mop-ups of Isabella's spilled water bucket, they yanked the last piece of tape from the drop cloth.

"Ready?" Maddie ruffled the plastic drop cloth and redirected his attention from the pleased twinkle in her eyes.

He nodded. "Born ready."

Starting at opposite walls, he and Maddie rolled plastic until they met in the middle. Hands touching, breaths mingling, and eyes locked, they stood victorious in the center of the beautiful pink room.

"We did it," Maddie whispered to keep from waking Isabella who'd curled up on a pallet in the corner an hour ago.

It was all he could do not to kiss the pleased smile below the drop of pink on her nose. "Hungry?"

"Starving."

"Should we wake her?"

"I may not know much about being a father, but I've learned this." He glanced at Isabella. "Never poke a sleeping bear." He took the wad of plastic from Maddie's arms. "If you'll put the brushes in some water, I'll see what I can rustle up in the kitchen."

"I make a mean grilled cheese." Her eyes sparkled.

"I remember the time you nearly burned down the parsonage fixing lunch for David and me. Blackest sandwiches I've ever seen."

"You ate every bite."

"A guy will choke down a lot when he's trying to impress a girl." Why had he said that? He turned before she could see the heat creeping up his neck. "I'll see if I have anything with some taste to it."

He was simultaneously pulling a skillet from the cabinet and mentally kicking himself for his bungling puppy-love-like comment when Maddie joined him in the kitchen.

She went to the sink and started rinsing the brushes. "Is Isabella having trouble adjusting?"

"Why do you ask?"

"She was so calm on the plane. I was kind of surprised when you said she's been getting into things."

He started chopping an onion. "She's eighteen months old. According to the books, that's what toddlers do."

"You've been reading parenting books?"

"Doesn't everybody?"

"I thought you'd know what to do…I mean, you've always been so good with kids."

"Never raised one before." He dumped the onions in the skillet. "Unfortunately, Isabella didn't come with an instruction manual."

"After trying to keep up with her today, I'm convinced it's every bit as hard as it looks."

He dug another onion from the bin and started chopping. "When did you get so insightful about kids?"

"Just because they don't like me doesn't mean I don't like them. I do."

"Isabella likes you. A lot."

Maddie shrugged off the compliment. "It's the granola bars I keep in my bag that she's really after."

"Isabella had just begun to bond with me and then I got sick. She must have been terrified when I left her." He glanced over his shoulder. "I can't thank you enough."

She pointed a wet paintbrush at him. "Guess my bedside manner doesn't repulse everyone."

He'd get sick all over again if it meant having her…no, he didn't have her. "I'm livin' proof you're one heck of a good doctor. The hospital that snags you will be blessed."

Maddie turned off the faucet. She pressed the last of the water from the bristles. "I'm not going to work in a hospital."

"Well, a medical practice then…I know you'll bless your patients. I'll even write you a letter of recommendation."

"I'm going to work for the Center for Disease Control…in Atlanta…at least I'm hoping to get the job."

"A lab?" His heart sank, not for him, but for her. "You've always been so adventurous. I guess I never pictured you stuck behind a microscope forty hours a week."

"I won't be stuck," she said with a bit of a defensive bite. "If there's an outbreak of some kind…I'll travel to the site, treat patients, and stay until the threat is contained. Then it's back to the lab to design proactive reoccurring protocols."

Where she'd be safe from real interactions. "When will you know if you're moving?"

"Soon."

Whether she was in Mt. Hope or in Atlanta, it didn't matter. Distance was distance. Miles or heart. "You really want this, don't you?"

"I do."

"Then I'll be prayin' that door swings open for you."

"Thanks." She lowered her eyes and dried her hands on a towel. "So, do you love Guatemala as much as you'd hoped?"

"More."

"High altitude is intoxicating."

"I remember when you came home from that summer you spent at the clinic. You were so pumped I thought you'd never live in the flatlands again. Miguel and Rosemary still talk about you."

Her smile dropped and he wished he hadn't brought up the couple Maddie had lived with during her stay in the village. "That was a long time ago."

"Sorry…"

"How are they?"

"They're remarkably well. Have gone on to have two more kids. Rosemary said she wouldn't have gotten through the grief of losing her baby if it hadn't been for you."

"Really? I felt so inadequate. If I'd had more training, I could have done something when their baby contracted that respiratory infection."

"The world's going to be a better place because you've got the training now." He was glad he'd restored her smile, even a forced one. If only he could restore the confidence losses had stolen from her.

"Maybe." She ripped a paper towel from the holder, spread it on the counter, and laid the brushes out to dry. "What you're doing, bringing fresh water to these people, is amazing."

He shrugged. "Makes me happy."

"Why?"

"You know how it is, the more we bless others, the more satisfied we feel." He stopped chopping for a minute. "Right after I arrived in the village, I heard about a young widow with two kids. I went to see what I could do. She was living on a couple of bags of rice some missionaries had brought by. The kids were skin and bones. She had a nice little piece of ground behind her little one-room shack. I helped her plant a few vegetables and taught her how to tend them. She and her kids have healthy things to eat every day now. She's managed to sell some of the excess produce and buy a few necessities. But she still has to carry water uphill for nearly a half mile. Just think what she could grow if I could get running water pumped up to her plot. Makes me giddy just thinking about seeing her standing at her garden with water shooting out of a hose." He realized he was babbling. "Bet you feel the same when you save someone's life."

A thoughtful smile spread across her perfect lips. "Yeah, it does."

"I remember how you used to light up when you got to treat a scrape or bruise at camp."

"That was a long time ago."

"Our calling never leaves us." He went back to chopping. "Now, no more distractions. I'm creating a masterpiece." He tossed another handful of onions in the skillet.

"Hey, go easy on the onions, mister. Your stomach is still tender."

"You can't expect a man to live on broth forever, doc." He looked over his shoulder. "It's time I introduce Isabella to my secret sauce sloppy joes."

"Do toddlers like tomatoes?"

"She'll have to learn to eat what I cook. I'm not spoiling my daughter."

Maddie shrugged. "My daddy spoiled me. And look how good I turned out."

"That settles it." He shoved sizzling onions around with a spatula. "No more late-night chocolate milks for Isabella. I'm not raising a princess."

"Too late." Maddie picked up one of the drying paintbrushes and swatted his back pocket. "You just gave her the perfect princess room."

"Hey!" Parker wheeled, spatula raised. "I love these jeans."

"Obviously. They still have the paint swat I gave you thirteen years ago."

"I remember calling that a low-down move."

"And I seem to remember that you deserved that smack." They stood there, watery paint and hot onions dripping on his old boots, as memories sharp as the smell of fresh paint and sizzling onions swirled around them. "Don't be such a baby, Parker. I'll buy you a new pair," Maddie teased.

"Don't want new jeans." He hung a thumb on one of the empty belt loops and acted like the spatula was a pistol he was whipping out of a holster and aiming at her. "These are my lucky Levis, lady."

"Lucky?"

"If I hadn't been wearing them when my friends threw me in the back of that truck and drove me to the hospital, I might have died."

"It wasn't the jeans that kept you alive."

"Sure it was." He took a step toward her, backing her up against the counter. "Made you come runnin'. If that's not lucky, I don't know what is."

Her eyes grew wide in disbelief and her perfect lips curved in fake protest. "Those jeans had nothing to do with me saving your sorry butt."

"Admit it. You've always loved how my butt looks in these Levis—"

The smile dropped from her lips and the curtain this easy banter had parted swooshed shut, cutting him off with blinding speed. He knew better than to venture beyond the boundaries she'd set for their friendship.

"Don't, Parker." She shook her head and pressed her hand against his chest. "Please."

He raised his spatula in surrender, blinking at the unexpected sting of tears. "Danged onions." Failing again to bridge the divide between them had left his emotions as vulnerable as typhoid had left his gut.

"Onions make my eyes tear up, too." And for the first time since their last goodbye, he saw tears in her eyes.

"You don't cook onions," he whispered gently.

"I cry when other people cook them. So there."

"Maa-d." Isabella came into the kitchen dragging a small blanket and rubbing her eyes. She lifted her hands indicating she wanted Maddie to pick her up.

To his surprise Maddie didn't hesitate. She zipped past him, swooped Isabella to her hip, and placed a kiss on her sleepy forehead. "You really need to get this girl a mother, Parker Kemp."

CHAPTER FIFTEEN

From the blanket Parker had spread under a gnarled mesquite, Maddie was enjoying their impromptu picnic and the peaceful view of his horse paddock. She pulled a blade of dried grass from Isabella's hair and laughed as the little girl devoured another bite of ground beef swimming in sweet tomato sauce. "I think she likes your cooking."

Parker offered his daughter a piece of fruit. "Controlling carb intake is key to ensuring a child's good health."

Maddie twirled the blade of grass between her fingers. "Is that what the books say?"

"According to my research—" he nodded in the direction of four horses grazing an overgrown paddock. "—raising kids is a lot like raising those beautiful creatures." Isabella grabbed a handful of meat sauce and smeared it on her bare belly. He sighed, grabbed the roll of paper towels and wiped away as much red as he could. He wadded the messy napkin and looked at Maddie. The gold flecks in his dark eyes sparkled like old times. "Go ahead, you can say it again."

"You've got your work cut out for you, buddy." She held the blade of grass up to the wind and let it go. "But Rome wasn't built in a day. Promise me you'll take it slow."

"Which part?"

"All of it, but especially the part where you try to become the perfect father overnight."

Isabella scrambled to her feet, toddled off the blanket, and picked up speed as she began circling the picnic spread.

"I'm afraid this one has only one gear…high." Parker held out his arms. "Come to Paki, Sugar Bean."

Isabella cut across the blanket, tipped over Maddie's soda, and launched herself toward him.

"Oh, no." Parker caught Isabella with one hand and snatched up the draining can. "Tell Maddie you're sorry you ruined her fancy jeans, Sugar Bean."

Maddie burst out laughing at the chaos. "She is her father's daughter." She pointed at the paint splotches on her knees. "Maybe you and I will start a new paint-splattered, wet-jean trend." She hopped up from the blanket, wiped her hands on her ruined pants, then started gathering the dirty plates.

"Leave 'em," Parker clambered to his feet and grabbed her hand. "Let's all take a walk."

Warmth zipped up her arm. "Walk?"

"That way the food can fall to our feet, and we'll have more room for dessert."

He'd said these same words to her the Thanksgiving after her father's death. She'd helped Momma fill the parsonage with friends, but she'd still felt so alone. So lost. Parker found her washing the dishes. He grabbed a dishtowel and stood beside her, telling her jokes and making her feel like she was a better person than she was.

Here he was doing it again. "I can't believe you're still touting that silly, old wives' tale."

"These size thirteens are all the proof I need." He raised a scuffed, paint-splattered boot then danced a little jig. His feet got tangled up in the blanket and he landed on his rear with a thud. "Since the rest of me is light as a feather that didn't even hurt."

Maddie hadn't laughed this much since that long ago Thanksgiving they'd spent washing dishes together in the parsonage. "Those clumsy boats are the very reason I allow my food plenty of time to digest."

"Come on." He waved her to him, and she hauled him to his feet. "I think it's time my daughter learned to ride a horse."

"She's only eighteen months old."

"And none of us are getting any younger."

"Hooses." Isabella took out cross the lawn.

"Whoa, little missy." He chased after his daughter, scooped her up, swung her around, then set her back on the ground. "Come on," he shouted to Maddie. "Let's introduce this girl to some of God's four-legged friends."

This realm fit him as comfortably as his scuffed boots and those silly worn-out jeans he refused to part with. To stay here was to risk falling under the spell of his easy, laid-back way of life. But she wasn't ready to leave the one person who loved her enough to tell her the truth, even when he knew it hurt. The woman she'd become looked nothing like the girl she once was.

"Wait for me." She ran after them.

His sly smile told her he knew she was finally running after that girl. "Hoof it, Maddie."

She caught up. "I haven't been on a horse since..."

"Since the day of your Momma's wedding." He wasn't the only one who thought about that night down by the lake. How they'd stood there under the stars and decided different fates.

"Maa-d." Isabella offered her hand for the walk across the yard.

Maddie glanced over Isabella's head. Parker grinned and began to belt out a rich baritone version of "Old MacDonald Had a Farm." Hand in hand, the three of them strode toward the paddock, Maddie harmonizing with the proper animal sounds.

Parker cut his long-legged stride to match his daughter's tiny steps. Patience had always been one of this giant man's most attractive qualities. At every new blade of grass, weed, or bug they encountered, he stopped the song, bent, and gave his child the scientific name of her discovery.

Listening to this man talk about nature was like listening to someone who believed the world would be a better place if everyone would simply take the time to enjoy God's creation. From the adoration on Isabella's face, this child grasped the wonder of his message.

The ding of Maddie's text alert broke the spell.

Parker swung Isabella to his shoulders. "We can wait if you need to check that."

"Could be the hospital calling about Etta May. I'm trying to talk her into having surgery, but she's not having it. You two go on. I'll catch up."

As Parker and Isabella eased up to the paddock fence, Maddie pulled out her phone and glanced at the screen. The message was from the head of the epidemiology department she'd interviewed with at the CDC.

The job is yours. We're partnering with WHO to shut down a cholera outbreak in Yemen. You're needed on site immediately. Grab your passport. You leave DFW in 24 hrs. Welcome to saving the world.

Shock turned into a tiny thrill. She'd done it. She'd reached her goal. Her hard work had finally paid off.

"Parker!" Maddie waved her phone as she tore toward the paddock. "Parker!"

Parker hoisted Isabella to the top rung of the fence. Holding firmly to his daughter, he turned toward the sound of Maddie's shrieking.

At the sight of his contented face, Maddie's excitement sank like a stone. She'd just reconnected with her friend, had even endeared herself to his child, and now she was leaving. Walking away before…before what? These two had totally captured her heart. Too late.

"Maa–d!" Isabella clapped excitedly. "Hooses."

"I see." She stuffed the phone into her back pocket.

"Good news?" Parker reached up and took hold of the tiny hand getting a little too close to a horse's curious mouth.

"Yes…and no."

Parker studied her for a moment, Isabella's bare feet beating against the fence slat. Pride swept his face. "You got the job, didn't you?"

"How do you do that?"

"Know what you're going to say before you say it?"

"Yes, that."

A grin the size of Texas spread across his lips. "Your face is easier to read than the Farmer's Almanac."

"You lost me on that one, cowboy."

"I hope not." His face was dead serious. He lifted Isabella off the fence and set her next to a bucket of oats and handed her the metal grain scoop. "Dig for treasure, Sugar Bean, while I talk to…Maa–d." He turned, then put his two big hands on Maddie's shoulders and looked her square in the eyes. "You're risk adverse. Which is crazy since you seldom fail. But staying safe doesn't mean you won't ever get hurt."

She wanted to bristle, but she was melting into the warmth of his accepting gaze. "You make me sound like a big chicken."

He inched closer, lowering his head toward hers. The familiar scent of Aqua Velva filled Maddie's nostrils and his gentle squeeze pumped her with courage. "You're the bravest person I know, Madison Harper. You knew what you wanted years ago. No matter what anyone said, you wanted to go to med school, and you went. You moved halfway across the country and learned to navigate those big cities…all by yourself. You flew to a third-world country rife with disease to pull a friend from the jungle. Anyone who knows you, knows you can do just about anything you set your mind to."

"Not everyone." The stone had risen to her throat, forcing her response into a whisper.

His brows knit. "Your mother knows your capabilities better than anybody."

Arguing the finer points of Momma's opinion of her would take away from what she really wanted to say. Had finally found the courage to utter. A burden she'd come home to relieve herself of once and for all. "I can't do everything, Parker."

He jammed his fists on his hips, daring her to argue. "Name one thing you can't you do."

She couldn't tell if she was misreading the situation, but something was pushing her to abandon her plan and take a foolish, crazy, irresponsible risk. "I can't love you, Parker Kemp, but I do. I always have." The truth sprang from her heart like a scared jack rabbit. It quivered in front of his growing smile. Before she could snatch it back, his fingers laced her hair and drew her lips to his.

His kiss was not the awkward peck of the love-struck boy who'd kissed her after their bike wreck. Nor was it the kiss of the dopey-eyed guy with a head injury she'd kissed after his truck plowed into a snowdrift.

Their lips pressed with uncanny accuracy. Alive with an urgency to reclaim the years they'd lost. His hands slid to her shoulders. Drifting purposely down her arms, his calloused palms found hers. As their fingers twined, Maddie felt the threads of their frayed relationship slowly knit together. His kiss deepened. His thumb turned in little circles in the soft skin between her thumb and forefinger, coaxing her beyond her wall of fear and into a world of possibilities.

The text alert sounded in her pocket. Probably more travel info. One more minute of bliss. One more minute in the arms of the man she loved before the ugly truth pushed itself between them: Mt. Hope didn't need an infectious disease specialist.

How could she hurt him again?

Her breath hitched, and she pulled away. "Don't fall in love with me, Parker."

"Too late." His lips brushed hers. "I fell in love with you the moment you waltzed into my Sunday school class." Parker's next kiss blew away the anxiety and filled her with the first deep breath she'd had in years.

Maddie's phone vibrated in her pocket. Someone was desperate to talk to her. Unwilling to face the heartbreak her decision would inevitably bring to them both, she ignored the warnings going off in her head. They could work this out. Somehow. Some way. Surely.

Parker was the one who gently broke their bond. He eased back and Maddie inhaled sharply as if she'd forgotten how to breathe on her own. The corner of his mouth turned up at the sight of her wide eyes. "You're beautiful," he whispered against her lips.

The phone vibrated again. Hopefully it was just Momma trying to reach her. She was the only person who kept dialing until Maddie eventually picked up.

He tucked a strand of hair behind her ear. "Could be important."

"Somebody better be bleeding." She released him, kissed the end of his nose, pulled out her phone, and scowled at the caller ID. "It's David."

At first, the rush of words her brother shouted from his end didn't make sense. Then suddenly they did. Every ounce of her training flew out of her head. And everything she'd never let herself imagine crashed in on her. "I'm on my way." She clicked off, her hands shaking, terror strangling her ability to say the impossible.

"Maddie?" Parker caught her as her knees gave out.

"Momma's car was totaled by a cattle semi. Charlie's transporting her to Mt. Hope Memorial."

CHAPTER SIXTEEN

Dust billowed behind Parker's old truck as they flew toward town. Maddie sat on the console, wedged between him and Isabella's car seat. She'd been on the phone since they left the ranch. She was all business on the outside, but on the inside, she was in no condition to drive and sort medical details. To Parker's surprise, she'd agreed to his assessment and allowed him to load both of his girls into the truck.

His girls.

Parker let his hand slide from the wheel and squeeze Maddie's knee. She was real. The kiss they'd shared was real. The love he had for her was so real it hurt.

She laid her hand on top of his, but her mind was focused on the conversation with Dr. Boyer.

Parker turned his concentration from planning their future together and back to navigating the road.

Maddie listened, shaking her head. "I'll be there in approximately two minutes Dr. Boyer, and that life flight better be on its way." She hung up, not happy with what she'd heard. "She's alive. Critical, but alive." She stared at the horizon, her face pale with shock. "Maybe I shouldn't have pressed the life flight?"

"Better safe than…you'll feel better once you've had a chance to assess her yourself."

"I'm not an ER doc. I…I…" She squeezed his hand. "Parker, what am I going to do if Momma dies?"

It was all he could do not to stop the truck and pull her into his arms. As much as Maddie had always tried to appear strong and independent, something in her wanted her mother's approval…even more than she wanted to be a doctor. If she lost another person she loved, she might never risk loving again.

"Start praying," he shouted over the ping of gravel hitting the undercarriage of his truck.

"I don't remember how," she half-sobbed.

"It's like riding a bike. You don't forget how, you're just a little wobbly when you first get back on."

"This coming from the guy who nearly killed me on a bike."

"The kiss was worth it." He glanced at her. "If you can't do it, let me."

She blinked back tears and nodded.

His silent pleas rushed to the throne while his truck raced to the hospital.

The tires squealed to a stop under the emergency room portico. "Go!" He jumped from the driver's seat and offered Maddie his hand. "I'll park then find you."

"Maa-d!" Isabella cried as Maddie shimmied out of the truck.

Maddie turned and hesitated.

"Go!" Parker shouted. "We'll catch up."

He parked the truck, freed Isabella from her car seat, and sprinted across the parking lot with his daughter in his arms.

Ruthie met him at the door. "Been prayin' since I got the call." She was still wearing a pencil behind her ear and carrying a big bag of burgers. "Any update?" she huffed for breath, dragging a greasy hand down the front of her apron.

The lump in his throat made it impossible to do more than just shake his head.

"God's got this." Ruthie took his elbow and led him through the automated doors.

The emergency room was buzzing with people who'd heard about the wreck via the Storys' phone tree. Nola Gay and Etta May were busy handing out hugs as Nola Gay pushed her sister's wheelchair around the waiting room. Howard had his arm draped over Maxine, who was sobbing like a baby about possibly losing her best friend. Betty Bob had been so distraught she hadn't bothered to whip up a batch of fudge. Roxie, still wearing her auto parts store polo shirt, was giving the receptionist what-for because she didn't have an update. Ivan had his reporter's notepad, but it was still in his shirt pocket. From the tears streaming down his face, it would be a while before he could write a word. Saul sat alone, stone-faced and rubbing his fist.

In the far corner, Maddie was talking with David and Amy. Parker ran to join their huddle. The second he was within reach of Maddie it was as if Isabella's sense of Maddie's anguish kicked in because she would not be restrained.

"Momma!"

Maddie opened her arms. "Come here, Sugar Bean." She patted Isabella's back. Hard to tell who was comforting who. "Go on, David."

David glanced from Maddie to Parker to his wife. The surprise on his face was evident, but he wisely kept his disbelief at the sight of a child clinging to Maddie to himself. "According to Saul," David continued. "Momma was bringing Romeo to visit the Story twins." His explanation came in short, terse bites. "The dog was riding in the front seat. Momma's pot pie was on the floorboard. Near as we can tell, Romeo must have gone for the pot pie. When she tried to stop him, she swerved into the lane of a cattle truck." He swallowed hard. "But we may never know exactly what happened."

"Dr. Harper." Dr. Boyer burst through their little circle. "We've got your mother stabilized. She's asking for you."

"She's awake?" Maddie's face was a mixture of relief and surprise.

"With all her injuries, all I can say is that it's a miracle I can't explain."

"I can." She turned to Parker and passed off Isabella. "Thank you." She looked at Dr. Boyer. "Can her husband come back?"

He shook his head. "Let's get her a little bit more stable first."

Before Parker could say a word of encouragement, Isabella burst into tears and the woman he loved disappeared behind a swinging door.

CHAPTER SEVENTEEN

Maddie drilled Dr. Boyer for facts as they strode toward the curtained bay and the sober-faced nurses hurrying in and out.

"The airbag's deployment saved your mother's life, but it also did some damage." Robin took her elbow and drew her aside. "The good news is that Leona doesn't seem to have any spinal or brain injuries, but…" he paused, giving Maddie a moment to brace for the worst.

During her residency she'd seen countless examples of what an exploding airbag could do. None of those images were comforting. "The bad news?"

"Leona has abrasions to her upper body, face, and hands. A broken wrist. Chemical irritation to her throat…and…a lacerated liver."

Why were they standing here chatting? "When does her life flight get here?"

He gave a little shake of his head. "According to the CT, it's a low-grade liver tear."

"But life flight's still coming, right?"

"No." He stopped her from bursting through the door. "It's nothing we can't handle here, okay?"

"If you think I'm letting a maternal-fetal specialist touch my mother's liver you've got another thing coming." The list of possible complications swirled in her head. "Screw this up and she could bleed out."

"Hence, the reason I'm going to do everything I can to avoid subjecting your mother to further trauma. For now, I'm ordering a non-operative approach."

"I'm not going to stand here and let you tell me that it's best to do nothing for *my* mother."

"We've done a CT. All we can do is wait, give the leak a chance to plug on its own."

"Wait? That's your medical advice? Do you understand that every second counts?"

"She's hemodynamically stable. The latest research strongly supports giving anything below a grade three 24 hours to repair itself. This course of action actually has a lower mortality rate than—"

"Maddie?" Her mother's voice sounded as if someone had taken sandpaper to her vocal cords.

"Get out of my way." Maddie pushed past him. She ripped the curtain aside and stopped dead in her tracks. "Momma?"

Swollen streaks of purple and dark blue had distorted Momma's face almost beyond recognition. Her left arm was tethered to an IV. Her right was stabilized with an inflatable brace from elbow to wrist. Momma managed to summon Maddie with the slight wiggle of the exposed fingers of her right hand.

Blinking back tears, Maddie squeezed past the nurse hanging a bag of fluid. "I'm here, Momma." Maddie wanted to crawl into her mother's bed and hold her. To say she was sorry. Sorry for not being a better pastor's daughter. Sorry she hadn't appreciated all the sacrifices her mother had made for her. Sorry for failing to find the happiness her mother had wanted for her. Sorry she'd pushed her mother away. Sorry she'd given up on God.

Afraid her touch would cause her mother more pain, Maddie stood immobile, not knowing what to say or do. Her mother needed the prayers of this entire town. She needed another miracle.

"Is Romeo okay?" her mother whispered.

The woman had nearly died, and she was worried about her dog. Although her mother was almost unrecognizable, it was her typical-selfless-Momma lying in this bed. Why couldn't she be more like her mother?

Momma's predictability was an unexpected comfort.

Maddie leaned in close. "Romeo's a little scratched up, but nowhere near as smashed up as you, or your car. Charlie put that hairy beast in the front seat of the ambulance so he could keep an eye out for possible internal injuries. You'll be proud to know that Romeo whined outside the hospital door until Charlie convinced the staff he was a therapy dog. The nurses have allowed that hairy beast of yours to sit in the waiting room. He's been a perfect gentleman."

"He's a good boy." Her mother's breaths were labored.

"He's had a good trainer."

Momma's lip twitched at Maddie's rare compliment. "Did I ruin my pot pie?"

A broken laugh escaped Maddie's clenched smile. "Peas and carrots are all over the highway."

Her mother scowled. "And it was one of my better crusts."

"Try to rest, Momma." Maddie stroked her mother's swollen fingers. "It'll help you."

"It's not true, you know."

"Dr. Boyer swears rest will heal the liver tear. But if you want to go to Dallas, just say the word and I'll—"

"Not the liver." Momma's head shook slightly then her face grimaced as if the tiny movement had sent a new wave of pain racing through her banged-up body. "It's not true what they say about your life flashing before your eyes as you die."

Tears stung Maddie's eyes. "Thank God you didn't die, Momma."

"Yes…God," Momma whispered. "It's all the things you didn't say that you think about. I begged God to let me have one more chance to tell you…" Her eyelids fell shut.

Maddie drew in a sharp breath, waiting for her mother to rouse. "Tell me what, Momma?"

The inhale and exhale of her mother's labored breaths roared in Maddie's ears, as if her mother was struggling to breathe for both of them. The sounds of beeping monitors and murmuring hospital staff disappeared.

Not knowing what else to say, Maddie leaned in close and whispered in her mother's ear, "Don't you dare die, Momma."

But her mother's eyes stayed closed.

CHAPTER EIGHTEEN

"Parker!" Nellie tackled Parker from behind, wrapping her arms around his middle and snagging Isabella's legs in the process. "I came as soon as I heard." Her seductive coo warmed his ear.

"Whoa, Nellie." He managed to wiggle free and stumble out of her reach. Every head in the waiting room turned their direction. They all knew she'd moved heaven and earth to help him. From their expressions, it was obvious they thought it was only natural for his appreciation to grow into a more serious attachment. Heat flushed his cheeks. Whether he'd kissed Maddie, and she'd kissed him back, didn't matter. He'd been vulnerable when Nellie dropped by the other night. If he'd encouraged her advances, then he was the one who needed to stop them, before she got hurt.

When he turned around, to his surprise, genuine crocodile tears slid from Nellie's green eyes. "Nellie? What's wrong?"

"Tell me what else I can do for you...and the Harpers." Sniffling, she held out a big bag filled with diapers, snacks, and everything he'd forgotten to grab for Isabella. "Mom called. When she told me you had the baby with you and not even an extra diaper, I ran to the store and picked up a few things, including some bland snacks for you."

Parker cast an appreciative nod toward Maxine. Her good intentions had put him between a rock and a hard spot…no, he couldn't blame Maxine. He'd put himself in this uncomfortable position by allowing Nellie to hope she could have his heart. His heart had been taken for years.

"That's real thoughtful of you, Nellie." He lifted the bag from her outstretched hand. "Maddie and I were so worried about Leona I just threw her and Isabella in the truck without a thought to how long we could be waiting here."

Nellie shut the waterworks off immediately. "Maddie was at your house?"

Letting Nellie down easy wasn't going to be easy. "She'd dropped by to deliver some pickles…" he nodded toward the Storys.

"Isn't Maddie the one who put you on that strict diet? I read the entire diet plan over carefully and it's going to be a while before you can eat something so acidic." Nellie suspicious eyes raked him from head to toe. She wasn't buying the doctor's innocent house call. "You have pink paint on your jeans."

"Yeah, I got the nursery painted. The color looks great. Thanks for your help."

"Like you, I never waste a minute when it comes to helping another." Nellie threaded her arm through his. "This little cherub deserves—" She gave Isabella's cheek a gentle tweak.

Isabella let out a pained cry then scrambled up his chest to higher ground.

Nellie's eyes widened in horror. "Oh, sweetie, I'm so sorry. Ranch work has taken a toll on my nails. Not that I mind." She kept cooing at Isabella, but she'd turned an apologetic gaze back on him. "I love helping your daddy." She let her gaze slide toward the door behind which Maddie had disappeared. "You two deserve someone who'll think about what's best for *both* of you."

"I appreciate everything you've done for my family, Nellie. Really, I do. But if I've misled you—"

"I'm just getting started." In a flash, her arms were around his neck, squeezing Isabella between them.

His daughter was squirming and fussing. "Nellie, Isabella can't breathe."

"You have no idea what all I intend to do to you...*for* you," she whispered. She rose on her tiptoes and planted her lips firmly upon his.

Isabella was crying and Nellie was kissing him hard when Parker's frantic eye movements caught a glimpse of Maddie coming through the swinging doors.

Her eyes met his. Her bottom lip dropped in shock. Her face paled then flushed red. Something had lit her fuse. If he were a betting man, he'd put his money on the red-headed spider spinning a web around him and his daughter.

****

The swinging ER door hit Maddie in the back as she watched Parker and Nellie kiss. She'd waited until Saul and David were finally allowed to see Momma before she'd rushed out to fall into the arms of her best friend. Deer-in-the-headlights terror widened his eyes when he spotted her.

In what appeared to be an attempt to preempt Maddie's misinterpretation, Parker clamped a hand on Nellie's shoulder and popped her loose.

He strode toward her, a whimpering Isabella holding tight to his neck. "Maddie."

Maddie held up her palm. "I don't know if Momma's going to live."

Parker refused to allow the distance she'd tried to create. He hooked her tight and pulled her close. It was like popping a cork on a bottle. Tears sprang forth and she buried her face into the warmth of him and Isabella.

"Hell's bells, darlin', Leona's not going to give up that easily." Aunt Roxie patted Maddie's back. "She's got more fight than a junk yard dog."

Maddie lifted her wet face. "Her liver's lacerated, Aunt Roxie."

David burst through the doors. "Maddie!"

She wheeled free of Parker's embrace. "What's happened?"

"They've rushed Momma to surgery."

David snagged her arm. "You can't go back there."

"Try and stop me."

He shook his head, his eyes huge. "They kicked us out when Momma's blood pressure dropped and her heart monitor went crazy. No family allowed." David's respirations were rapid. "You're *family*, Maddie. Not her doctor."

Unspoken understanding passed between them. If they lost their mother, they would both be lost.

Her big brother needed her moral support. And she needed his.

Etta May cleared her throat and drew Maddie's attention to the group that gathered around them like a chain-link fence of protection. What Momma meant to each person in this room was written on their heartbroken faces.

Maddie offered David her hand. "We're *all* family."

He pulled her into a big hug. They held each other and cried while everyone in the circle held their breath.

Maxine pressed a tissue into Maddie's palm. Aunt Roxie gently laid a hand on each of their shoulders and led David and Maddie to two empty seats. Everyone shifted to make room for Amy to slip in on David's side and for someone to join Maddie. Her teary eyes found Parker and he instantly moved in beside her. Isabella, sensing Maddie's distress, cried to go to Maddie. When Parker tried to hold her back, her cries grew louder and more insistent.

Maddie held out her arms. Isabella shimmied free of Parker and lunged into her grasp. Maddie clutched her tight. Isabella's scent was a pungent mix of paint, horses, and sloppy joes, but it was a sweetness Maddie had never experienced. She rubbed Isabella's back, surprised at how quickly the action soothed them both.

She loved this child. A lot. How could she? She'd only known her a few weeks, but she couldn't have loved her more if she'd carried her for nine months and given birth to her.

Then it hit her. If this incredible tugging at the heart for Isabella's welfare was even a fraction of what Momma felt for her, no wonder her mother had refused to die.

CHAPTER NINETEEN

Maddie hung up the waiting area phone and turned to relay the update from the OR. "Momma's bleeding internally. They're searching for the source. It could be the tear. It could be a rupture they've yet to find."

"What does that mean?" Saul's voice cracked.

Maddie couldn't bear the lost look in her stepfather's eyes. He'd risked love…twice. He deserved many good years with a good woman. "Momma's in big trouble," she whispered. "And it's my fault."

"How is it your fault?" David demanded. "You weren't driving the car."

"She was coming to the hospital."

"We were the ones who requested a pot pie," Nola Gay argued.

"I knew we should have just eaten the okra and let it run its course," Etta May added.

"Momma was coming to talk to me." Maddie's tears were building. "I was awful to her the last time we spoke. I think she was coming to—"

"Listen here, young lady." Saul strode across the room and set his hands firmly on Maddie's shoulders. His usually charitable eyes blazed with a fire that dared her to argue. "Your mother believes you and David are the best thing since sliced bread. There's not a single thing either of you could ever do to change her mind." The flame flickered out and he relaxed his grip. "Now, I need you to tell me anything you can about this surgery and what it means for your mother. Please."

No wonder Momma loved this man.

Maddie swallowed and took Saul's hand. "I'm not a surgeon, but I'll do my best."

Everyone crowded in.

Maddie wished they weren't hanging on her every word and waiting for her to tell them everything would be fine. She couldn't make that kind of promise. The body was so intricate. She couldn't guarantee that once the surgeon got inside that Momma's injuries wouldn't be too extensive to repair. In the end, she opted to give the simplest version of her best guess. She kept the list of fatal possibilities to herself.

Saul listened intently, taking in every detail. By the time she finished, his grip on her hand had tightened so much she couldn't feel her fingers.

For a few moments no one said a word.

Romeo padded across the waiting room, his tail limp. He laid his head in Saul's lap. Saul absent-mindedly patted the dog's head. "Romeo thinks we should pray."

Maddie stroked Romeo's soft ear. "Momma said he was a smart dog."

"Not here." Saul gathered Romeo's leash. "In your father's chapel."

Maddie flinched at the thought of darkening the doors that resembled the church that had killed her father. But if she was granted the opportunity to set things right with her mother, she first needed to have a conversation with God. "I—"

Saul stood. "You don't have to come, Maddie."

She rose to her feet. "I do."

Parker offered her his hand while holding Isabella's with the other. Saul and Romeo started down the hall. Everyone followed like captives being led out of Egypt. When Parker, Maddie, and Isabella finally caught up with the little mob, Maddie saw that everyone was standing outside the chapel. Saul held the heavy wooden door open, but no one had gone in.

Maddie left Parker and Isabella. "What's wrong, Saul?"

"Someone's praying," he whispered.

As Maddie took a step toward the door, a woman shot from the chapel and ran smack into her. Maddie steadied them both by placing her hands on the woman's shoulders. "Freda?"

The nurse's head shot up, tears streaking her face. "Sorry, Dr. Harper." She backed away and hurried down the hall.

Maddie went after her. "Miss Freda, are you okay?"

She stopped and sniffed. "Just heard about your mother. Had to come say a prayer for her...and for you."

Maddie's mouth fell open at Freda's sincere concern. "Thank you, Freda."

"I love your daddy's chapel." She nodded toward the door where everyone was filing inside. "Your parents were the only ones who knew about my husband's drinking. Killed him eventually, but not before he put me in the hospital a few times. When the chapel was finished, Leona gave me a key in case it was ever locked and I needed a place to leave my burdens." She pointed at the verse engraved above the door. "Matthew 11:28. One of my favorites." She started quoting, "Come to me..."

Maddie took her hand and joined her. Together, they finished Christ's promise of rest for those who felt like they couldn't carry their burden another step.

Freda's smile was rusty, but it took on a warm and tender glow by the time it reached her eyes. "I always knew you'd done your memory work. Why'd you always pretend you hadn't?"

"Why didn't you tell me about your husband?"

"You were a child. And by the time you came home a doctor I so ashamed at how difficult I'd made your life. My pride wouldn't let me admit my wrong. Pride's a hard master. Don't let it ruin you." She marched toward her post.

Pondering the warning, Maddie turned to find Parker and Isabella waiting patiently outside the chapel door. Everyone else had filed in, including Nellie.

Parker's eyes dove deep into her soul. He saw her fears, but instead of judgment there was compassion. "We can pray out here."

She shook her head and threaded her arm through the one he used to support Isabella. "It's time I got back on that bike. God and I have some catching up to do."

Parker kissed her temple and opened the heavy door.

Stepping into the chapel was like coming home. Not a place—like the town of Mt. Hope, her old bedroom in the parsonage, or even the church where she'd grown up. But a feeling of security and love…the feeling she used to have whenever she was wrapped tightly in her father's arms.

The miniature version of Mt. Hope Community Church had three short pews on each side of a carpeted aisle. At the front of the sanctuary, Momma had recreated the stained-glass sunburst behind a cross that had always given Daddy a halo as he delivered his Sunday sermons. Beneath the beautiful scene, Saul knelt with his head bowed and his hands lifted. Romeo sat quietly at Saul's side as if he, too, knew this place was special.

Nola Gay had parked Etta May's wheelchair beside their regular seats on the second row on the right—widow's row—Momma had always called the twins' favorite spot. Bette Bob and Ruthie had squeezed in with them. Maxine, Howard, and Nellie had claimed the head elder position on the second pew on the left. Ivan sat alone, his camera and notepad respectfully tucked away. Roxie stood at the back, not sure where an Episcopalian fit in, but obviously as taken with Momma's attention to detail as Maddie. David and Amy huddled together on the front row, their heads bowed and David's shoulders bobbing up and down with uncontrollable sobs.

Maddie walked the aisle, her arm coiled through Parker's. She tapped her brother's shoulder. "Have room for me?"

David wiped his nose on his sleeve and scooted closer to Amy. "Always."

Maddie, Parker, and Isabella squeezed in. Flanked by the brother she adored and the man she loved, Maddie lifted her face toward the stained glass. She felt as if she was standing at the foot of the path that led to the cross surrounded by shards of glorious light. She'd made so many mistakes. Had no right to expect God to welcome her back, let alone hear her plea to save her mother. But the verse she'd just repeated with Freda kept spinning in her head. She *was* weary. Weary of fighting, of running, of pretending she was stronger than she was, of pushing away everyone who'd ever dared to love her…including God.

She closed her eyes and whispered, "God, I've no right to ask you to forgive me, but my parents aren't here." Her breath hitched at the possibility of losing Momma forever, too. "Please, God. Forgive me." She sobbed into Parker's shoulder. He stroked her hair and Isabella patted her hand.

Peace settled into the raw places and warmed Maddie from the inside out. She drank up the relief like a thirsty traveler. Resting in comfort, she dared to silently ask one more thing. "And God, whatever you decide to do about Momma, go easy on her. I've been hard enough to handle. She deserves a break."

Relieved to have finally started a conversation with the Lord, Maddie continued her silent spilling. She told God about the job in Atlanta, the upcoming assignment in Yemen, and how she couldn't bear to think of leaving Parker and Isabella. She was moving through the list with such concentration that the sudden sound of Parker's intoning, "When peace like a river…" startled her.

His smooth, calming voice filled the chapel. Etta May and Nola Gay were quick to join in, followed by Maxine and Howard. David cleared his throat, squeezed Maddie's hand, and added his tenor to the beautiful mix in the chapel's perfect acoustics.

The lump in Maddie's throat dissolved. She opened her mouth, not sure what would come out. It had been so long since she'd sung a hymn. Her "It is well…" bumped into Parker's baritone with a raspy gasp.

He smiled at her and the last of her angst melted away. When the song ended, the power of the music still remained. Whatever happened, Momma had done what she'd always excelled at doing—she'd brought people together. She'd brought Maddie home.

Saul's shoulders lifted. He rose and turned, looking stronger and resolved. He gathered Romeo's leash, gave Parker a grateful pat on the shoulder, then strode from the chapel. One by one, the others filed out giving Maddie, Parker, Isabella, David, and Amy a moment to themselves.

While Maddie was certainly feeling better about her relationship with her Lord—and even the outcome of her mother's surgery—God had not given her a clear answer on what to do about pursuing the CDC job. "Parker, would you mind taking Amy to get some coffee? I need to talk to my brother."

Parker and Amy exchanged curious looks, but both of them recognized the siblings' need to be alone.

Once the chapel had completely emptied, Maddie squeezed David's hand. "No matter what happens with Momma, we're going to be fine, right?"

"I love you, Maddie. I always have."

"I know. I'm sorry I let my envy of your favored-son status push us apart."

From the arch of his eyebrows, he was seeing her for the first time. "It's not easy living in someone's shadow."

In turn, she saw him. He was no longer just an older brother who'd been a hard act to follow, but he was a man who carried a similar weight on his own shoulders. She'd never considered how difficult it had been for David to try and fill the place of the man everyone adored. "There are worse things."

They stared at the stained glass, their clasped hands like an anchor in this storm.

"David, I need your advice."

He reared back, his brows knit in surprise. "This is a first."

"I'm serious."

"Okay," he said warily.

No sense putting it off. "I've been offered the job in Atlanta."

"That's great!" He wrapped her in a bear hug. "Momma's gonna be so proud." When he let her go, he saw the angst on her face. "What am I missing here?"

"I have to leave in a few hours."

"What? Why?"

"There's a cholera outbreak in Yemen."

"Tell them your mother's been in a wreck. Surely, they'll let you delay your departure a few days."

She shook her head. "Time is of the essence."

"So, you asked for my advice, but you've already made up your mind?"

"Not completely."

"Because?"

"I love Parker."

She could see his heart breaking for her. "Oh, Maddie." He pinched the bridge of his nose. "And he loves you."

She nodded. "How can I work this out, David?"

His expression was sympathetic and soft. "I can't believe when you've finally asked for my advice, I've got none to give." He patted her shoulder. "This is between you, Parker, and God, little sister."

CHAPTER TWENTY

Isabella had fallen asleep on Parker's shoulder while he and Amy walked the hospital corridors in search of a vending machine. They returned to the chapel with three bags of chips and two bottles of water. Nellie was waiting outside the closed chapel door.

She waved and smiled as they approached. "It's Isabella's nap time, Parker."

He kept a protective hand on his daughter's back. "Looks that way."

"Why don't you let me take her back to the ranch and put her down for a good rest?"

He shook his head. "I like holding her."

"But—"

"He said no, Nellie." Amy had acquired the requisite pastor's wife smile in the few years she and David had been married, along with a kind but firm delivery. "Shirley's at the parsonage keeping my kids. If you really want to help, I'm sure she would welcome the relief."

Nellie's cat-like eyes drew into angry little slits. Her suspicious glance at the closed chapel door implied they were hiding something. "I'd love spending time with your angels, Amy, but I just remembered I have an … appointment." She spun in her high wedges and let her long legs carry her far away from an unbearable evening of unrewarded childcare.

"I owe you one," Parker said after Nellie was out of earshot.

"Tell me why Maddie wanted to talk to David." Amy sipped water, eyeing him carefully over the edge of the bottle.

Parker shrugged, but a sick feeling churned in his gut. She probably wanted to tell David about her job offer and work out her mother's care if she couldn't delay her departure for Yemen.

"You know what she wanted—" Amy's eyes narrowed. "—you just don't want to say."

"It's not mine to tell."

"David's going to walk out that door and tell me everything she said, so what will it matter if it comes from you or him?"

Amy was right. When two people really loved each other, they didn't play stupid games. They were honest and upfront, and they didn't leave the other one to guess if or when they might finally be together.

He let out a sigh. "She got the job in Atlanta."

"That's great!" Amy sobered at his somber expression. "Great for her, but...not so much for you, right?"

"Is it that obvious?"

"Parker, a person would have to be blind not to see how much you have always loved that girl. Have you told her?"

"Yes."

"And?"

That moment he'd held her in his arms, he couldn't even breathe let alone sort through the mountain of logistics. "She loves me, too."

"Oh, Parker." Amy clapped her hands like she was already planning her sister-in-law's wedding. "That's wonderful. Leona's going to be so happy. Maybe we should bust into the operating room and tell her. Seeing Maddie happily married to you would give her another good reason to fight."

He rubbed his palm over Isabella's back. "The CDC wants Maddie on a plane to Yemen tonight."

Amy's smile fell. "What about Leona?"

He shrugged. "It's got to be Maddie's decision."

David exited the chapel, saw Amy, and strode past Parker. His eyes were red. David slipped an arm around his wife. "Any word on Momma?"

"Not yet, sweetheart. They'll want to make sure they've located every possible bleed. Could take a while."

"I need some coffee." He turned and clapped a hand on Parker's shoulder, careful not to disturb Isabella. "Sorry, man. My sister's a—"

"Good woman," Parker whispered.

"That too."

Parker held Isabella a little tighter as he watched David and Amy walk away hand in hand. He and Maddie would have a different relationship if she continued flying around the world and he returned to his water project in Guatemala, but they could meet up every few weeks. He loved her and she loved him. They could make it work.

A few minutes later, Maddie emerged from the chapel. She was scowling at her phone. The peace he'd seen on her face during her quiet reflection on the cross had evaporated.

"Bad news?" He asked.

She stopped, startled to hear his voice. Her attempt to flash him a small smile was her way of saying she was pleased and sad. "I have to leave in ten hours if I'm going to make this flight out of Dallas." She showed him the CDC text with her flight info. The attached itinerary. And the HR forms she could fill out at the airport and email before boarding her plane. "David thinks I'm being selfish."

"Did he say that?"

"He didn't have to. I could see it in his eyes."

Pieces of Parker's breaking heart lodged in his throat. "David's calling is different than yours."

She reached up and gently stroked Isabella's sleeping face. "I don't deserve you, Parker," she whispered as her lips brushed his.

He wasn't sure what that meant, but he was glad to see that despite the angst on her face now, the time in the chapel had served her well. She'd come to peace with the Lord and, from the loving way she was looking at his daughter, she'd accepted his decision to be a father. With the right amount of support, he prayed she would eventually come to peace with her mother, but most importantly, with who she was.

"Let's go back to the waiting room so you won't miss any updates from the OR." He offered his hand.

Maddie threaded her fingers through his. "Parker, I don't know how this is going to work out."

"One day at a time, Maddie. A day at a time." He kissed her forehead. "We'll figure it out."

The same folks who'd been holding vigil since they'd received word of Leona's accident had returned to the waiting room.

Maddie was the one who noticed Nola Gay had pushed Etta May's wheelchair away from the group. "Etta May looks uncomfortable. I need to get my patient back to her room."

He shifted Isabella's sleeping body. "She won't want to go."

"They both seem to adore your charms. Will you try?"

"I'm better with weevil invasions."

"You're great with those two old women and you know it." She tugged him across the room to where Etta May was rubbing her jaw.

"Etta May," Maddie squatted beside her wheelchair. "Are you having trouble breathing?"

"She's been huffin' and complainin' of being dizzy since we left the chapel," Nola Gay wrung her hands.

Maddie took Etta May's wrist and checked her pulse. Rapid. "Etta May, do feel pressure on your chest?"

"Who wouldn't, with these cantaloupes?" The elderly twin rubbed her lower cheek and grimaced. "But it's my jaw that feels like it's about to fall off. I must have been talking way too much." Her breaths were labored, and it was all she could do to bring her other hand to her stomach. "Sister, I might embarrass myself and throw up."

"You didn't sneak a piece of okra, did you?" Nola Gay snatched a near-by trash can. "Here."

"Can't breathe." Etta May plowed her head into the waste bin and retched blood.

Maddie grabbed the handles on Etta May's wheelchair. "Parker, tell the nurses I need help." She looked around but Parker was already sprinting to the desk. "Possible pulmonary embolism," Maddie shouted after him.

By the time Parker had rounded up a nurse, Maddie was already wheeling Etta May through the ER bay's double doors. "I need IV blood thinners and a doctor who knows how to break up this clot. Stat!"

Parker latched on to Nola Gay's elbow and did his best to balance her and his daughter as they ran to catch up. Maddie pushed Etta May into a bay and wheeled around. Together, Maddie and the nurse lifted Etta May onto a bed. When Maddie wheeled and spotted Nola Gay clutching the trash can and Parker holding Isabella, who was wide awake and on the verge of crying because of the commotion, Maddie gave a terse order to the nurse, "Get them out of here."

Parker was so mesmerized by how easily Maddie maneuvered in this world of life and death that he couldn't move.

"Now!" Maddie demanded.

Parker nodded, took Nola Gay by the hand. "Let's give Maddie space to work, Miss Nola Gay."

"Me and Sister came into this world together." The elderly twin planted her feet and nodded her head toward her sister's bed. Etta May's lips were blue, and her eyes were closed. "I won't let her leave this world alone."

Maddie gave a few more clipped orders then ripped the curtain closed between them.

CHAPTER TWENTY-ONE

Parker led Nola Gay to the waiting area. "Can I get you some coffee, Miss Nola Gay?"

She shook her head. "I ain't been alone a moment in my life."

"And you're not now." He meant God, but from the way she clung to his arm, he knew she wasn't letting him leave either. He held the chair while Nola Gay slumped into it. "Maddie's good at what she does. If anybody can—"

"She's too good to be wastin' her talents on the likes of us," Nola Gay agreed. "Sister and I have always known this dusty little town had nothin' to offer a girl with her kind of dreams. Leona did everything she could to rein that girl in, but Sister and I knew it was only a matter of time until that girl broke loose. Maddie Harper was born for bigger and better things." She lifted her thick glasses toward Parker. "Better than any of us."

Her pat on his knee cut the rope on the wild horse he'd wasted years wishing he could tame.

CHAPTER TWENTY-TWO

Maddie had just finished settling Etta May in the ICU when Dr. Boyer sent her a text that he'd be out shortly to talk to her family. The adrenaline rush that had successfully diverted her guilt at what had happened to Etta May plunged. Maddie's knees went weak. What might have happened to this dear old woman if the twins hadn't insisted on being in the middle of everything? Momma's accident, Parker's kiss, the CDC's job offer had been distractions, but that did not excuse her lack of attention to her patient. She'd totally dropped the ball on Etta May's follow-up.

Maddie updated the chart.

Nola Gay stuck her head in the room. "How's my sister?"

"Let me come to you." Maddie stepped into the hall. Parker and Isabella flanked Nola Gay with a supportive grasp. Parker returned her appreciative smile with a rueful nod she didn't understand. She gently took Nola Gay aside. "Etta May's suffered a blood clot to her lung, but she's a tough one."

"Thank you for being here, child." Nola Gay wiped a tear from her cheek. "I think the Lord sent you home just for me and Sister."

Maddie shook her head. "I failed her, Nola Gay. I should have insisted Etta May have that filter installed when the blood thinners weren't getting the job done."

"She didn't want surgery."

"But as her doctor, I should have—"

"No one can make Etta May do a darn thing she don't want to do. She may seem all sweet, but she's tougher than an old dill pickle." Nola Gay's arthritic hand cupped Maddie's cheek with grace she did not deserve, and rarely offered to others. "We all take risks. Sometimes they work out, and sometimes they don't. But me and Sister are livin' proof that stayin' safe is a surefire guarantee of a very boring life."

Humbled by Nola Gay's easy forgiveness, Maddie realized she had some forgiving of her own to do. "You're two of the least boring people I've ever met."

"Well, imagine how excitin' we might have been if we'd married and had children. Our children might have been embarrassed by our antics, but our grandchildren would have loved us."

Maddie laughed. "That's for certain."

"Life's too short not to forgive yourself for today's mistakes and risk it all for tomorrow's happiness, child."

"Thank you, Nola Gay." Maddie kissed her cheek, but her gaze was on the handsome cowboy and the beautiful little girl asking to go to Momma. "I think the Lord brought me home to hear that very piece of wisdom." She pecked Parker on the lips and asked him to wait while she situated Nola Gay in the chair beside Etta May's bed. Before she left the twins, she promised, "I'll come back the minute we have information on Momma. You need anything?"

"Go. We don't want you to miss a word of what that city slicker doctor has to say," Etta May said weakly.

"You're good at this, Maddie." Parker said as they hurried back to the waiting area. "Real good."

His sincere praise, although tinged with a touch of melancholy, was better than an adrenaline rush. "Thanks." Maddie swallowed and looked at her watch. They had less than five hours together…unless…

Unless she didn't go.

The idea, strangely enough, wasn't a door slamming on her dreams. It was a window opening to a whole new way of thinking. She was good at what she'd trained to do. She wanted to use those talents. Choosing Parker didn't mean she wouldn't, she would just use them in a different way. She didn't know how that would look. All she knew for sure was that she could no longer ignore the Holy Spirit's nudging to take a very drastic turn. Whether her mother lived or died, she was destined to make her life wherever Parker Kemp made his.

She couldn't wait to tell Parker, but she didn't want to do it in the middle of a hospital. She wanted one last privacy. The joy of seeing his face when she told him she was going to kiss him for the rest of his life belonged only to her.

They rushed to the waiting area, where the people who'd loved her and her family for years congratulated her on saving Etta May.

"She's brilliant. A blessing to the medical community." Once again Parker's praise was a mixture of pride and resignation.

The pride she loved. The resignation she intended to blot out. But just as she was about to approach him with an invitation to find a private corner, he set Isabella down and let her run to his mother, who'd joined the growing crowd.

"Are we too late?" Maddie's grandmother shouted as she and Cotton rushed through the sliding glass doors.

"Cotton!" Maddie ran to the door and threw her arms around the white-haired church janitor who'd swept her grandmother off her feet. "Grandmother!" She fell into her grandmother's embrace.

David joined in the welcome and between the two of them, they quickly updated their grandparents on the details of Momma's wreck, the internal bleed, the risks of surgery, and Etta May's pulmonary embolism.

"This town may be small," Grandmother said, "but it is never dull." She kissed Maddie's cheek. "I'm glad you were here, dear."

"We all are." David patted the empty chair beside him. "You got time to take a load off, little sis?"

Maddie smiled. "I do."

David squeezed her knee and whispered so only Maddie could hear, "The sick of this world are going to be lucky to have you."

Parker deserved to be the first to hear of her change of heart. And then Momma. For now, she would let David think she was going. "As the lost of this town are to have you, big bro."

Dr. Boyer came through the swinging doors. When he lowered his mask, Maddie had never been so relieved to see his cocky smile. "Leona did well in surgery. We located the bleed and managed to seal it."

"Only one?" Maddie asked.

"Only one." Dr. Boyer assured her. "I'm expecting nothing less than a full recovery."

Cheers went up and the desk nurse gave everyone a shushed warning. Maddie and David snatched a quick hug. Then David turned to his wife and Maddie threw herself into Parker's arms. He spun her around. When he set her down, he said, "Go see your Momma. I'll take you back to your car when you're ready. No hurry."

"I hate to make you wait. I know Isabella has had enough of the hospital."

"She can go home with Mom."

"All right." Maddie couldn't wait to remove that sadness from his eyes. "Give me a few minutes."

Maddie and David accompanied Saul to one of three recovery bays. Momma was attached to tubes and monitors. She was groggy but her coloring was much improved. She asked again about the status of her pot pie, and they all laughed.

"She's back," David said.

"Thank God." Saul gently lifted Momma's cast-free arm and kissed her hand.

A dopey grin slid across Momma's mouth. "You can't get rid of me that easily, Saul Levy."

"Then I'm the most blessed man alive." He kissed her hand again.

A lump formed in Maddie's throat. Being loved and loving someone back was worth the risk. And it was what she wanted more than anything, even more than becoming an epidemiologist with the CDC. "Momma, I've got to check on Etta May and then—"

David shook his head, his wide eyes warning her to stop. "We're all going to let you and Saul have a minute. Right, Maddie?"

"Sure," Maddie agreed. "You rest, Momma."

Outside Momma's room, David led Maddie away from the door. "I'll tell her you had to catch a plane once she's a little stronger." He pulled Maddie into a big hug. "Go save the world, little sis."

She couldn't contain the joy bubbling inside of her. Momma was going to be fine, and she was going to tell Parker she was staying. She'd update David later, but for now, she had to find the man she intended to spend the rest of her life adoring.

After a quick duck into a restroom to splash water on her face and fluff her hair, Maddie hurried to the parking lot.

She found Parker waiting at his truck. She ran to him and wrapped her arms around his neck. "Miss me?"

"Always." He peeled her loose without a kiss and opened the passenger door. His sober resignation stung. She'd give him a chance to make it up to her when she had him alone. She put a booted foot on the truck's running board and started to hoist herself in, then stopped.

The car seat and Isabella were both missing.

"Where's Isabella?"

"Mom's taking her to see Dad for a few hours."

Disappointed she wouldn't have an excuse to squeeze in beside the adorable geek turned irresistible hunk, Maddie climbed into the passenger seat. Parker closed her door. Drinking in the faint odor of Aqua Velva, she watched him stride around the truck's front bumper. He seemed tired, or sad, or both. The day had been long, and he was still recovering from a severe illness, but something wasn't right. She hoped the serious look on his face had everything to do with her fighting cholera in Yemen.

When he opened the driver's side door, she waved a hand over the pristine leather. "I was so upset about Momma I didn't notice your clean truck. What happened to all the almanacs, fertilizer sacks, and Spanish dictionaries that used to litter your floor?" she teased.

"Decided the best way to keep up with Isabella was to get my act together." He climbed behind the wheel. "Don't look so skeptical. People can change, you know."

Despite niggling worry, she couldn't help the grin spreading across her face. "I do."

If he'd caught her meaning, it didn't register on his face. She didn't blame him. He believed she was leaving him…again. Once they arrived at his ranch, she intended to wrap her arms around his neck and tell him death would be the only thing that could separate them. Then she'd hold on to what she wanted for the rest of her life.

But on second glance, she couldn't stand the hurt in his eyes any longer. "Parker, I—"

He cut her off. "I can drive you to the airport if you want to leave your car in Texas until you get back in the States."

Enough with the long-suffering attitude. Why didn't he put his foot down and beg her to stay? "How would I get my car to Atlanta?"

"Maybe your mom and Saul will feel up to bringing it to you in a few months."

"A few months?"

"No one cures cholera overnight." He cut a pointed glare her way. "Not even you."

"You wouldn't bring my car to me?" She reached over and laid her hand on his leg. "If I asked real nice." She felt him flinch.

"Maddie…" He started to say something, but his bobbing Adam's apple cut off his words.

He was nervous. He'd been physically clumsy around her before, but she'd never seen him afraid to talk to her. To tell her what he was really thinking. Was he going to ask her to marry him? Was that the reason for the change in his demeanor? Was his reluctance tied to his belief she was leaving? Couldn't he see from the way she looked at him that she couldn't wait to say yes?

Yes, I'll marry you, Parker Kemp.

Heart swelling two sizes in anticipation of him slamming on the brakes and pulling her into his arms at the happy news, she managed, "Parker?" Her fingers pressed above his knee. "What is it? Tell me."

He swallowed again. "While you were taking care of me, I loved watching you work. It was a thing of beauty to see you move so comfortably in *your* world." His chocolate eyes were watery. "You can spot a medical problem as easily as I can spot a corn weevil."

"That's romantic."

"Hear me out, please." He turned his gaze back to the road. "I'm gifted with agriculture. You're gifted at healing. We're both too gifted to waste our God-given talents."

"I don't plan to waste mine. Do you?"

"You would if you stayed in Mt. Hope because of me."

"Are you staying in Mt. Hope?"

"This isn't about me or what I do or do not do for Isabella's sake." His knuckles whitened on the steering wheel. "I think you should go to Yemen without any ties."

She released her hold on him. "Oh, you do, do you?"

"I do."

"What if I was to tell you I'm not going?"

His head jerked toward hers and the truck headed for the ditch.

"Parker!" she yelled.

He quickly corrected before a single tire left the road. "You've got to go."

"No, I don't."

"But—"

"There were two perfectly qualified candidates in the running with me. I'm sure either one of them will be happy to jump in and take my place."

"You're scared right now, Maddie. Your mom almost died. Your favorite patient almost died. And you're worried I might relapse. Those aren't good reasons to change your plans."

"So, you think I would be happier if I walked away from everyone I love?"

"Dr. Boyer expects your mother to make a full recovery. Etta May's on the upswing, and—"

"They're not the reason I'm staying."

He shook his head and pressed the gas. "I can only concentrate on one thing at a time, and I need to concentrate on raising my daughter." He was driving faster, like he couldn't wait to get her out of his car.

"This isn't a Bible quiz where you must get all the answers right, Parker. We can—"

"*We* can't."

"I thought you loved me."

"That's why I'm letting you go."

CHAPTER TWENTY-THREE

M addie fluffed the pillows propping her mother's back. "That better?"

Momma eyed her over her reading glasses. "About as fluffy as they were five minutes ago."

Maddie searched the room she'd tidied twice today already. "Need anything?"

Her mother removed her glasses. "There is one thing you can do for me."

"Sure." She'd already cleaned up from lunch and finished two loads of laundry. If she had to put Romeo through his obedience paces one more time she was going to go out of her mind. "What is it?"

"Quit hiding out and get on with your life."

"Momma, you're still recovering."

"It's been two weeks since Dr. Boyer released me from the hospital."

"He said you should take it slow."

"Slow, not immobile. You've waited on me hand and foot. If I need anything, I have Saul." Her eyes cut to the open French doors that overlooked the dock where Saul sat twiddling his thumbs. "It's not good for a man to feel useless."

"He took care of one dying woman and—"

"Which makes him more than capable of taking care of me. And for the record, I'm banged up...not dying."

"Are you throwing me out?"

"How far could you go? You sold your car."

"Cotton left the keys to his truck. Said I was welcome to it while he and Grandmother were off on their European riverboat cruise."

Momma put her book and glasses on the nightstand. She patted the bed and Maddie obediently sat beside her. "Are you sure you can't get that job back at the CDC?"

"I don't want it." Not that she didn't care about the suffering in Yemen. She did. She just couldn't quit thinking about the suffering in Guatemala, especially if Parker made some crazy decision to never go back there.

Momma studied her intently. "Did I ever tell you that I almost didn't marry your father?"

The pain meds must have loosened her mother's tongue. "No."

"Your father and I were so different. I was a serious journalism major with plans to spend my life writing. Your father was loud. Charismatic. Incredibly sure of himself...except when he wasn't." Momma swallowed hard. "I loved that man so much it hurt. But I didn't see how we could possibly work out our differences. I just knew I'd regret the rest of my life if we didn't try. So, I agreed to elope. Some days were easier than others. Church work took a toll on your father. He'd disappear for hours. It wasn't until I married Saul that I learned your father hid out at this very lake." She shook her head sadly. "Our whole marriage, I'd believed J.D.'s struggles were my fault. To compensate for my failings, I demanded perfection from you and your brother. Not because you weren't already perfect in my eyes, but to protect you from any negative critiques." A tear slid over her bruised cheek. "How foolish. Your father didn't need perfect children any more than he needed a perfect wife. He just needed us."

"Momma—"

Her mother held up her casted hand. "When you're young, the days are long. But as you grow older, you realize the years are short." She raised her eyes to meet Maddie's. "Too many years have gotten away from you and me, sweetheart. God has given us a chance to claim the remaining days."

Maddie snagged an anxious breath. "I'm listening."

"I was so determined to be nothing like my mother, that I went as far as I could on the opposite end of the spectrum." Her voice broke. "I understand your desire to swing the pendulum the other way."

The idea that she'd behaved exactly like her mother had once done came as a shock. But it was true.

Everything Maddie had done, including her brief relationship with an Olympic half-pipe snowboarder and her refusal to go to church, had been to prove she was nothing like Leona Harper.

If Momma noticed how this honest peek in the mirror had both humbled and horrified her, Momma didn't let it keep her from what she was determined to say. "When you started needing some space, as all girls eventually do, I panicked. I held you under my thumb."

Maddie shook her head ever so slightly, afraid the tiniest movement would bring the wall down she'd guarded for years. And then where would they be? Maddie knew how to do distant. Close terrified her. "Momma, you didn't."

"I did, sweetheart." A tear dripped from her mother's cheek. The glistening drop landed like a sledgehammer to glass. The barrier between them shattered in the space of a heartbeat.

A slight smile tugged at the corner of Momma's healing lip. She seemed relieved, yet still completely determined to totally clear the air. "I was afraid of what your father, the church, this town, and even God would think of me if you took a wrong turn. I'm so sorry

I didn't trust you to manage your own life. You've proven yourself very capable again and again."

Overwhelming love pushed past the last of Maddie's resentment, anger, and bitterness. "Momma, I'm the one who should be apologizing. I've always known you'd walk on water for me."

Momma chuckled at Maddie's reference to her old mandate to *save Momma* should the family car ever plummet over a bridge, but Maddie knew it was the thawing of her heart that had really pleased her mother.

Momma squeezed Maddie's hand. "If you'd allow me one last word."

"Don't you always have the last word?" Maddie teased, truly thrilled to discover that the woman who'd successfully fascinated and irritated her for twenty-nine years wasn't perfect. And, best of all, Momma no longer expected her to be perfect either.

"Living with purpose liberates you. It's risky, but worth it." Momma brought Maddie's hand to her split lip and tried to form a kiss. "Your purpose doesn't look like mine, my love. Live the life God intended for *you*."

Maddie didn't fight the tears. She'd come home to close things up tight. Had given herself four weeks to put her life as the repressed, small-town pastor's daughter behind her once and for all. She'd come to grips with the town, with God, and now her mother. Why on earth couldn't she come to grips with the fact that she and Parker would never be more than friends? Especially, now that he had a child. She would make a horrible mother but, strangely enough, Isabella had been on her mind nearly as much as Parker these last few days. Raising that little girl didn't scare her nearly as much as the thought of losing Parker forever.

"What do you want, sweetheart?"

"I don't know what I want, Momma. And I've always known what I wanted."

"And you've always gotten it." Momma lifted her chin with her finger. "You know why?"

Maddie shook her head.

"You were born with your tight little fist raised in the air and a defiant look in your eye. Anyone who got in your way would eventually eat your dust."

"Nothing like falling face-first to get a mouthful of the stuff."

"That can happen when you risk loving someone."

"I don't like failing."

"Failing doesn't kill us." Momma's eyes filled with compassion. "But not getting up and trying again will."

Momma had done just that. Got a job, sorted Daddy's finances, moved out of the parsonage, remarried...all of it must have been so hard and Maddie had been so wrapped up in herself she'd been absolutely no help.

Tears spilled down Maddie's cheeks. "I don't know how."

Momma took her hand. "Parker has always wanted what you wanted."

"What's that?"

"To save the world," she paused then added carefully, "He and Isabella are going back to Guatemala."

"How do you know?"

"Maxine."

"By which you mean Nellie's been spending time out at his ranch." Every hair on Maddie's neck rose like a dog determined to protect its territory. "I'd like to see that pampered spider navigate the jungle in those heels." When their laughter died down, Maddie asked, "What should I do, Momma?"

"I'm done telling you what to do, Maddie."

"Okay, tell me what *you* would do."

A tiny smile tugged her mother's lip as she pondered what to say. "Well, I've heard that in countries where typhoid is endemic, the most important action is to secure safe drinking water and disposal of sewage."

Maddie's brows knit in confusion. "So?"

"For someone who's brilliant, you have a hard time sorting the trees from the forest."

"Just tell me, Momma. Please."

"Until they get clean water in Guatemala, they'll need good doctors, right?"

"You're the one who's brilliant, Momma." Already planning for the obstacles Parker would throw at her and strategizing for ways to overcome them, Maddie jumped to her feet. "Where's the key to Cotton's truck?"

Momma lifted her blanket and pulled out a single key. She held it up with a sly smile. "Someone's got to be that little girl's mother. I believe you're the perfect woman for the job."

"How do you always know exactly what I'm going to do?"

"Oh, my little one. You'll always be *my* baby."

Maddie snatched the key. "I love you, Momma."

Chapter Twenty-Four

M addie shifted Cotton's truck into high gear. Windows open and her hair whipping around her face, she flew down the quiet country road. The small plot of land Parker called a ranch waited on the horizon. She hoped he was waiting for her.

She pulled into the drive and jumped out before the dust settled. A rich baritone version of *I've Got Friends in Low Places* floated from an open window. To her relief, Nellie's car wasn't parked in the drive. Maddie bounded toward the back porch then ground to a halt on the bottom step when Parker appeared at the screen door.

"Maddie?" His pleasure seemed quickly replaced by the conviction that he'd done the right thing in letting her go. He flipped the dishtowel over his shoulder, opened the screen, and stepped outside. "So, it's true? You didn't go to Yemen? Did they grant you an extension?"

"No." Behind him Maddie could see Isabella playing with blocks on the blanket they'd used for their wonderful picnic. "I didn't ask for one."

"Why not?"

She stuck her hands in her front jean's pockets, stalling for the best way to get this conversation going. "I'd forgotten to tell you how good I thought you were in a crisis."

"What crisis?"

"Grandmother falling down the stairs."

Suspicion gathered his thick brows. "That was four years ago."

"Right. And I never said thank you." Maddie tried to concentrate on the golden flecks in his eyes instead of the butterflies in her belly. "Nor have I thanked you for taking over after I heard about Momma's accident. You were right. I was in no shape to drive. And then when Etta May had her pulmonary embolism, you knew exactly what to do."

"Guess I should have gone into medicine."

"No!" She took a step forward and he took a step back. "You're exactly where you belong. I was just trying to say…we make a good team."

His eyes narrowed. "You could have texted me."

She was making a mess of this. Failing again. "Well, not exactly…"

"Why?"

Get up. Momma's words pushed her closer. "Text messages can be misinterpreted."

Parker planted his feet and crossed his arms. "We have talked this to death, Maddie. We haven't been a team since our Bible Bowl days."

"We were number one in our region. We could have won the Bible Bowl Nationals if I hadn't let you down."

"Why are you really still in Mt. Hope, Maddie?" He lifted an open palm and waved it like he was giving her the floor.

"Whether or not I wanted things to change after Daddy died…they did. Momma left the parsonage, married Daddy's lawyer, and made a new life for herself on the lake. David gave up being a perpetual student and began applying all that knowledge to our father's pulpit. And me…I turned my back on everything that had ever mattered to me. God. Family. You."

He shook his head. "Maddie, don't."

"Just hear me out." She took a determined breath. "You're a clumsy geek who'd rather spend his time ridding Etta May and Nola Gay's garden of corn weevils than perfecting your basketball lay-up. You'd rather cook and sing and charm people like Momma into believing you have a heart as big as this West Texas prairie than tell me the truth."

"And what is the truth?"

"There's enough room in that huge ticker of yours for that precious little girl *and* an uptight epidemiologist who can't cook, scares away most children, and still has big dreams of saving the world."

"Is that all?"

"No! I think you should go back to Guatemala."

"Not that I need your blessing, but Sugar Bean and I are heading that way as soon as I find a buyer for this place and raise the money to go back."

"I'll buy it."

"What?"

"That way the ranch will be here when *we* decide it's time to come home."

"We?" He glanced over her head, his eyes landing on Cotton's truck. "Where's your car?"

"I sold it."

"Won't you need a car to drive around Atlanta when you're not off saving the world?"

"I sold the Porsche because I won't need a *sports* car in Guatemala." She pulled out a wad of cash. "I think this will be more than enough for an all-terrain vehicle, don't you?"

He stepped to the edge of the porch, his nostrils flaring. "How did you get the CDC to send you to Guatemala?"

"Are you not listening? I'm not going to work for the CDC." She took a bold step toward him. "I'm sending myself to Guatemala."

He stepped down one step. "You can't go to Guatemala."

She stepped up one step. "I've had my shots. I'm over twenty-one. And I've seen what they have for doctors down there. They need me. And frankly, you need me, Parker."

"Maa-ma!" Isabella had toddled to the screen door. She plastered her face against the screen and raised her hands to signal her need to be held. "Maa-ma!"

"Did you hear what she just called me?"

"She's confused."

"That little girl needs me." Maddie's gaze held his as she pointed toward Isabella. "Look through your child-raising books. I'm sure it has a chapter or two on the importance of having a maternal influence."

Gold flecks swirled in his eyes. "I was sitting in my third-grade Sunday school class when a beautiful blonde first-grader walked in holding tight to her big brother with one hand and her mother with the other. The new pastor's wife asked Miss Freda if David and Maddie could be in the same class until they settled in. 'It would make the transition easier for my little girl,' she said. Miss Freda snarled and said, 'she supposed just this once it wouldn't hurt.' But it did hurt, it hurt you bad. I saw you flinch at her judgment and raise your chin. You were terrified, but you weren't about to let anyone know. You marched to the front row, took a seat, and stared straight into the eyes of Miss Freda. Your older brother scrambled after you, but you were just fine." He'd grown into his Adam's apple, but it still bobbed slightly under the weight of this memory.

"I knew right then that you were something special," he continued. "A girl willing to face down her fears to get what she wanted…even the fear of being someone's wife and someone's mother." He descended the last step between them, now only towering over her by a head. "Sugar Bean's hungry."

Maddie lifted her chin in a mock show of defiance. "Want me to make grilled cheese?"

"If this is going to work, you have to promise you'll *never* make me eat another grilled cheese." Before she could tell him he had a deal, he scooped her up and drew her close. "I love you, Maddie Harper. I always have."

She melted against his big frame, burying her nose in his thick neck and the comfort of Aqua Velva. "And I've always loved you."

Over his shoulder, Maddie could see Isabella's eyes widen, as if she wanted to be in the middle of this joyous moment.

"Paki," Isabella pounded the screen.

"Hang on, Sugar Bean. I've got to kiss your maa-ma."

"For the rest of her life." Maddie smiled up at him and stroked a strand of dark curly hair from his brow. Then she turned her head toward the door. "And we're both going to kiss you, little girl, until you get so big it embarrasses you as much as my momma and daddy used to embarrass me."

Parker and Maddie's lips found each other with ease. The fit was perfect, as if they were a couple who'd been kissing each other their whole life. Which, technically they had been. But this time was different. They were not kissing because one of them was bleeding, or sick, or terrified. This kiss sealed a promise. They would always be there for each other, but especially when they were bleeding, sick, or terrified.

Loving someone and being loved back was exactly as Momma had said—intoxicating and liberating.

Epilogue

T wo years later

Leona had found the sparse Guatemalan airport signage less than helpful. But the lack of mileage signs on this twisting mountain road the jeep rental guy swore would lead to Parker, Maddie, and Isabella's village terrified her. Not once had Parker mentioned the dangerous ruts or thousand-foot drop-offs.

She'd always longed for adventure, but four-wheeling third-world mountain switchbacks wasn't exactly what she'd had in mind.

Leona squeezed little Jamie's legs draped across her lap. "David, are you sure this is the right road?"

"Saul's in charge of the GPS." David shifted into a lower gear. "Hang on, there's a big boulder up ahead. We're gonna have to hug the edge."

Without a single seatbelt in this rusty vehicle, every pothole posed the risk of sending somebody flying. If they flipped over the edge, they'd all be lost.

"Maybe we should have let Parker come get us." Amy's vice grip on little Libby hadn't deterred the child's enjoyment of this bumpy carnival ride.

"It would have spoiled the surprise Parker has planned for Maddie," David shouted over his shoulder.

Saul pointed at the waterfall to their right. "No wonder our kids don't want to live in West Texas. It's beautiful here."

Leona would have smiled at Saul's use of the term *our kids*, but the continual jostling was as unsettling to her stomach as the river that fed that waterfall. Sooner or later, they would probably have to cross water.

"Not getting much of a signal." Saul waved his phone around, gave up, then dug out the printed pages of Parker's directions. "Once we get past the boulders, Parker says we need to keep an eye out for washouts because cars have been known to drop into those cracks and never be seen again." Saul grinned and looked over his shoulder. "How you doin' back there, sweetheart?"

Leona grabbed the side of the open jeep and hung on. "Do we have to cross over any of those swinging vine bridges?"

Saul looked at the paper. "Maybe."

"Tell him the rule, David," Leona shouted over the motor.

"What rule?" Saul asked.

"If the car goes over the bridge and lands in the water, first thing we're all supposed to do is save Momma." Her son shifted gears again and gunned the motor. Black smoke coughed out behind them.

Saul reached back and squeezed Leona's knee. "So that's why you've been taking swimming lessons?"

"We live on a lake," Leona said. "It's a safety issue."

While her son and husband had a good laugh at her expense, Leona savored the healing that had come to her family. It hadn't taken more than a mere mention of a family vacation to convince

David and Amy to join her and Saul in surprising Maddie the week
before she was due to deliver her first baby.

Leona had been nearly as excited at the prospect of finally having
her whole family together again as she was at how close David and
Saul had become. And while she hadn't seen Maddie and her little
family since the wedding, Maddie had made a point to FaceTime
every family dinner night. They'd all grown closer than ever.

It hardly seemed possible that it had been two years since Leona
had actually hugged her daughter's neck and sent her off to live in
the far reaches of Central America.

She would never forget the night Maddie returned from Parker's
ranch with that dreamy smile on her face and announced that she
and Parker had decided to go to Guatemala together and they were
leaving in a month. Tempting as it was to say *I told you so,* she'd
wisely kept her mouth shut. She and Maddie had put their heads
together and pulled off a beautiful wedding in the church where
Parker and Maddie had fallen in love.

Of course, it helped that Leona had a few favors she could call in.

Roxie had arranged an expedited dress hunt in Dallas. Ruthie
took over the catering of the reception…burgers, beans, big slices
of meringue-covered pie, and even brought in Angus to operate
her chocolate shake machine. Etta May insisted that she was up to
helping Nola Gay supply the pickles plus a bushel of fresh roasting
ears. Ivan Tucker took the photographs and put his most beautiful
shot of Parker and Maddie kissing under an arch Saul built on the
front page of the Mt. Hope Messenger. Mother and Cotton flew
Melvin in from the condo they'd bought him in Belize. He stopped
in Abilene, picked up the stretch limo, and had it shining like a
jeweled ostrich egg. Maxine threw the biggest bridal shower Leona
had ever seen. And Nellie surprised everyone when she showed up
at the rehearsal dinner with Dr. Boyer in tow.

The ceremony was almost as perfect as Maddie. Her long blonde curls framed her bare shoulders in the simple, yet elegant silky sheath. The moment she tried it on, Leona knew she didn't care how much the dress cost, it had been designed with her daughter in mind. Nothing to tie the girl down, not a trace of the ruffles and lace Leona used to make her wear, and a fit as perfect as the man Maddie had chosen to spend her life serving beside.

Wilma Wilkerson played the organ. Jamie and Isabella were the cutest little ring bearer and flower girl anyone had ever seen. David performed a touching ceremony, only stopping to embarrass his little sister once. Parker held Maddie's hands and sang a song so beautiful everyone was crying long before the last perfect note floated to the rafters.

But the memory Leona treasured the most, the one she played in her mind again and again, was the tiny moment while she, Maddie, and Saul were standing at the back of Mt. Hope Community Church waiting for the ceremony to begin. Saul was making sure they had everything they needed before he was going to take his seat. Leona was adjusting Maddie's veil when Maddie turned to her and said, "I wish Daddy was here, Momma."

The lump had been in her throat all day, but at that moment it was all she could do to say, "So do I, sweetheart. He would be so proud."

"I know." Maddie blinked back tears. "But he's not here. And I know Daddy would want us to live." She'd turned to Saul and offered her hand. "Will you stand in for my daddy?"

It was the happiest moment of Leona's life as all three of them walked the aisle together.

An especially jarring bump shook Leona out of her reverie. After two hours of hanging on for dear life as their jeep struggled with the climb and the hairpin turns, they finally sputtered past a few ramshackle houses built out of anything the poverty-stricken residents could scavenge.

David brought them to a stop at a small, cinder block structure where several people patiently waited in a line that stretched out the door. Some held children who were obviously not feeling well. Others had leg or arm injuries. And one supported the elbow of an elderly woman.

Leona smoothed her hair. "Is this the hospital?"

"Only one way to find out." David crawled out, took Jamie from Leona's lap, and offered her assistance as she unfolded herself from the back seat.

They walked into a well-lit room that had one exam table and smelled of disinfectant. Maddie was wrapping a bandage around a child's leg while Isabella was busy coloring at the little table and chairs Leona had shipped last Christmas. Maddie's swollen stomach stretched her scrubs to their limits. She was tired and hot, but her face glowed with contentment.

"Nana!" Isabella, a beautiful three-year-old with shiny black curls, leapt from her seat and bounced across the room. "It's Nana and Papa!" She flew into Leona's arms.

Maddie looked up from her patient. "Momma? What are y'all doing here?"

"I've never missed an important moment in your life, and I don't intend to start now." Leona kissed and hugged Isabella. "Besides, I need to see my beautiful granddaughter."

"You need to share." Saul held out his arms and Isabella lunged for him.

The family spent the rest of the afternoon doing what they could to help Maddie. They knew she wouldn't leave until every patient had been tended. Watching her daughter work filled Leona with wonder and an intense sense of accomplishment.

"You're good at this, Maddie." Leona kissed her cheek. "Are you glad you took the risk?"

"Absolutely." In the flash of Maddie's smile, Leona saw remnants of J.D. Instead of making her cry, it thrilled her to know his legacy had been multiplied a hundred times over.

By the time they'd finished at the clinic, Parker had returned from a day of releasing the first clean water into the village well.

It was a night of celebrating, laughter, and pure joy. Leona loved seeing how happy Maddie and Parker were and how perfectly their little family of three fit together.   After David and Amy retired to put the kids to bed, Parker took Saul on a tour of his innovative water project.

Leona and Maddie stood side by side washing the dishes, just as they had so many times at the parsonage kitchen sink. "I'm writing a big check and I want you to build whatever you need to improve the health conditions of these people."

"Momma, you don't have to do that."

"I want to." Wishing she'd done it sooner so Maddie would have a first-rate facility to deliver her baby, Leona handed Maddie a rinsed plate. "Getting nervous about the delivery?"

"Not really. Women here do it all the time without much help."

"Then why so quiet?"

"What if screw up my kids?"

"You will," Leona laughed. "That's a given."

Maddie elbowed her. "Thanks for the vote of confidence, Momma."

"Isabella is thriving. I don't think you have to worry, but just in case, let me tell you a secret." Leona dried her hands and took Maddie's hands in hers. "You and David were both born so perfect. I spent years trying not to mess you up. And yet, I did."

Tears slid down Maddie's cheeks. "Momma, if I can do half as good a job as you did raising us, my children will be blessed."

"Hopefully you'll do a better job than I did of letting go."

"I'll always be your baby, Momma. Promise you'll never let me go."

"Never." Leona wrapped her arms around her daughter and released the flood pent up in her as well.

These were not sad tears. These were tears of victory. They'd all been through so much and had come so far since J.D. died. None of them had wanted things to change...but they had...especially in the hearts of each one of them.

She'd become very comfortable and confident walking in her working shoes. David had found his own stride in filling his father's shoes. And Maddie had exchanged her designer heels for hiking boots and baby shoes. The transformation suited her God-given purpose perfectly.

The Harper family may have walked through the same valley in different shoes, but they'd never walked alone.

The End for the Harpers...or is it?

Afterword

Aren't the people of Mt. Hope fun? If you've just discovered this series via **BABY SHOES**, you'll be happy to know that you can get your hands on the three preceding books along with the final book in the series, a Christmas story called **SANTA SHOES**.

Here's your opportunity to catch up. Start with **WALKING SHOES**.

Did you enjoy **BABY SHOES**? **YOU** can make a **BIG** difference when it comes to spreading the word about these stories.

Reviews are the most powerful tools in my arsenal when it comes to getting attention for my books. When loyal readers share their enthusiasm and their reviews, it is secret gold to a book's ranking. I'm very grateful every time a reader tells their friends about this series and leaves a review. I'm grateful for you, dear reader.

Let's connect on FaceBook @AuthorLynneGentry or via my website, www.lynnegentry.com, so you'll always be the first to know about new releases.

Thanks for joining the Harper family on this leg of their Mt. Hope Southern Adventure.

I hope you'lltake a moment and sign up for my occasional newsletter. You'll be the first to know of new releases, plus you'll get your FREE copy of the first ACT of my audio performance of this story. Sign up @ www.lynnegentry.com and start collecting all three audio acts.

INTRODUCING MY NEW SERIES

If you loved the folks in Mt. Hope, then you'll want to grab the first book in my newest WOMEN OF FOSSIL RIDGE series and slip away to the Texas Hill Country. These books explore the real-life struggles families can face as parents age. The Slocum women are tough, funny, and stubborn. You'll laugh, cry, and root for everyone in this emotionally packed, inter-generational tale.

Twenty-five years ago, the Slocum women buried their mother-daughter relationship in the Frio river and went their separate ways. Sara and Charlotte manage to pretend their weekly long-distance calls are the extent of their obligation to each other until another lapse in Sara's judgment causes her to break her hip. Now Charlotte must drop everything and fly to Texas. Charlotte's short-term caregiving plans are dashed when she realizes her aging mother needs long-term care. While Sara struggles to regain her independence, Charlotte grapples with the impossible task of juggling a slightly demented mother, a high-pressure job, and a rebellious teenager daughter.

But unless these two women can release the fossilized secret sandwiched between them, the next generation will never fly.

The Women of Fossil Ridge Series is a touching addition to the small town, generational series of favorite authors like Ann B. Ross, Jan Karon, and Beth Hoffman.

SNEAK PEEK OF *FLYING FOSSILS*:

Chapter 1
Sara: An Independent Mother

As usual, you're being overly dramatic, Charlotte Ann." I hug the phone receiver between my ear and shoulder, stretch the cord across the kitchen, then snag a butcher knife from the wooden block.

"Putting a few dents in a lawnmower is hardly a reason for me to give up my ranch."

"Mother, you totaled a two-thousand-dollar *riding* mower!" My daughter's anger crackles on the line. "What if you'd been hurt?"

Contrary to Charlotte's insinuations, I'm not some fragile, rusty weathervane easily spun by the changing winds that sweep through these Texas Hill Country valleys. As per the invariant order of things, my feet have become deeply rooted in the rocky soil. I'm attached to this land tighter than the fossils that cling to the banks of the Frio River.

For forty-two years, I've been the mother. Charlotte the child. Simple laws govern our parent-child relationship. I'll admit, there are rules that allow for an orderly transition of power, if that sad time should ever come. But, I'll not be pushed into speeding things along simply because it suits Charlotte.

Trading roles with my daughter now would be like winter unexpectedly giving way to fall. Buds waiting to bloom would shrivel and die. There'd be no crops to harvest. Birds would never head north. Nothing would ever be right again. I know, because twenty-three years ago I was forced to go against the expected order of life. It was a tragedy that has ruined everything.

"Mother, did you hear me?" Somewhere in Charlotte's aggravation, I hear the little girl I used to know, the one who sat beside me on the piano bench...frustrated that she was having difficulty mastering Twinkle, Twinkle Little Star...worried that she never would.

I shift the receiver and whack a Bartlett pear into tiny pieces. "Don't worry, I'll pay you back."

"You know this is not about the money!" Charlotte barks.

"Then why did you bring it up?" I ignore my daughter's huge sigh and slide a piece of fruit through the bars of my ringneck parrot's cage. "Here you go, Polygon."

My bird waddles his perch shouting, "God save the Queen."

"Loyal and smart." I say as I wiggle the pear enticingly. "You need more roughage in your diet, my feathered friend. Can't have you getting backed up again."

"Mother, could you please stop talking to that blasted bird and finish our conversation?"

Polygon hops off his perch, wraps his claws around my arthritic knuckle, and begins to peck at the fruit. Touch is the sensation of touch I miss more than conversation. Which is strange, considering the complaints I lodged with Martin when I felt worn out by the constant pawing of third graders. Guess that goes to show how easy it is to take something for granted until it's gone.

I release the fruit and Polygon waddles toward his seed dish with a full mouth. "At least my bird listens."

Charlotte sighs. "I bought the riding mower to help you. The doctor said the strain of *pushing* a mower over that huge yard is putting your heart at risk." Her continued exasperation rattles me more than her exaggeration. "Obviously, power equipment isn't the answer."

"Anyone could've confused all those fancy pedals."

"You're seventy-two, Mother." She always manages to cite my age before overstepping the boundaries we've set in place. "There's no shame in admitting that you can no longer keep up with three hundred acres of rugged hill country."

I wipe the window with the sleeve of my robe and gaze at the pasture dotted with patches of this spring's fading bluebonnets. "No one was hurt."

"This time." The strain in her voice is as irritating as a mandatory fire drill.

"You want me to let the place grow up around my ears?"

"Of course not." She sighs to emphasize the stress I'm obviously adding to her very busy day. "But since you refuse to consider a move, I have to hire you some help."

I bite my tongue. Silence won't end this conversation with Charlotte, but it won't hurt her to believe it's the only defense I have left.

"I'm worried about you, Mother."

Charlotte's deep inhalation is my cue to take a seat because the recounting of my shortcomings that she feels honor bound to recite has grown into a rather long list. "In the last six months, you've flushed your dentures down the toilet."

"Just the lowers."

"You got lost on the way to town."

"Winnie found me and hauled me back home." I add, "Long before dark."

"I hate to think what would have happened if you hadn't run out of gas along her mail route."

Overstated dramatics always harden my resolve. Ask any child who was unlucky enough to have me as their teacher. "No law against trying a change of scenery."

"You don't like change, Mother," my daughter snips. "That's why we can't seem to have an honest and productive conversation about your future."

I sink into the chair and rest my elbow on the table. "Just because you think the old gray mare *ain't* what she used to be…" I cringe at that I've resorted to using slang. "…that doesn't mean I want to leave my home of forty-five years and move to Washington, D.C., Charlotte Ann."

Surely it wasn't that many years ago that Martin and I ignored a weathered *No Trespassing* sign, climbed an old, barbed-wire fence, shed our clothes, and jumped from a thirty-foot bluff with the abandon of two people with more nerve than sense. The moment our naked bodies slid into the crystal-clear water, we knew the Fossil Ridge Ranch was meant to be our little piece of heaven.

I've loved and lost on this land. I can't bear to leave any of it.

"I know this is hard," Charlotte whispers.

"How *could* you know? You only come home once a year."

"Mother, that's not true. I've flown to Texas four times since Thanksgiving. And if you don't start cooperating, I'm going to have to come home in April as well."

Without following the school calendar dates scramble in my head. "Four times?"

"Yes," she says. "I have a job, a teenager, and a marriage I'm trying to keep together. I can't keep dropping everything to..."

Her pause is my cue to say something that will soothe her conscience, to grant a pass that lets her off the hook. That's been our unspoken agreement for twenty-some years. I don't get a pass. She doesn't get a pass. That way neither one of us has to forgive the other. Slocums are like that. Charlotte may have taken on that fancy McCandless surname when she married a good-for-nothing playboy, but roots deep as ours are tougher than weeds to yank out.

Charlotte's quiet. But I can hear her ripping the tiny gold treble clef back and forth on the thin silver chain around her neck. She's gearing up to issue my ultimatum. I suppose I should take some consolation in the fact that she still wears the little trinket I gave her years ago. Perhaps we're not completely lost to each other.

"If you want to stay on the Fossil Ridge, then you'll have to give this new guy a chance."

"He's already mowed over the bluebonnets in my front yard. They're beautiful this year, but he cut them down before they could seed. Next thing you know, he'll be toppin' my myrtles."

"I'll text him to be more careful. Please, for my peace of mind, can you just give this new guy a try?" Charlotte's breathing is becoming more rapid. Any minute she'll blow, unable to leave well enough alone. "That's all I ask."

"That's all?" Anger pumps through my veins and I spring from the chair, a taut rubber band aimed at the class bully. "If you call stripping my independence *guarding my heart*, Charlotte Ann, I'll take my chances with high cholesterol and a push mower."

I hang up the phone with a decisive slam and march to the counter. Sticky juice oozes from what remains of the mutilated mound of fruit.

Whatever happened to family taking care of family? My neighbor LaVera's grown son takes care of her. Bo isn't pressuring his mother to leave her place, nor does he pawn off his responsibilities on hired help.

I swallow a bite of the vanilla-sweet flesh then poke a sliver through the bars of the birdcage. "Charlotte won't be satisfied until I sign over complete control of *my* life."

My bird abandons his preening and snatches his breakfast with his bright red beak.

"Sweet Moses," I snap. "Say something, Polygon!"

I know better than to encourage this feathered chatterbox to speak with his mouth full, but this traitorous deed by Charlotte has me in such a stew I'm willing to risk the undoing of my bird's etiquette training.

For once, Polygon behaves and remains silent. Although pleased the hours I've invested in my parrot's behavior has finally begun to pay off, I admit that at this very moment a word of encouragement, even a feathery nod would be a comfort. How many years has it been since I've had someone in my corner?

More than I care to count.

The screaming kettle gyrates above the gas flame. "We'll show Charlotte who can still take care of themselves, won't we, Polygon?"

I pour boiling water over a twice-used tea bag then wait for the water to brown. It's maddening that my life has come to recycling tea bags. Martin and I had planned to spend our golden years spoiling a passel of grandchildren. I shuffle to the fridge. My gnarled finger traces the photograph that curls beneath the World's Best Teacher magnet stuck to the door.

The little beauty sitting beside me and Charlotte is my only grandchild. Aria was eight when this photo was taken nearly five years ago. I haven't seen this little lioness in months. Busy teenager stuff, her mother claims. But I can't help but wonder if Ari has also outgrown her need for me. After all, she's probably taller than me by now, and well-past the age of appreciating anything I could teach her. And I'd planned to teach her so much. Her times tables. Piano scales. How to tell a barn swallow from a sparrow. The best way to free a fossil from the limestone that lines the river.

Some dreams are best forgotten.

I return to my tea, splurge and add a cube of sugar, then lift the rose-patterned porcelain cup to my lips.

My apple-green bird tilts his head, his beady eyes assessing my brewing storm. I blow steam in his direction. "You won't leave me, will you, Polygon?"

"C'mere." He waddles the length of his perch. "Pretty girl."

I rest the cup on a saucer and stick my finger through the wires and stroke the soft down above his beak. "If only family were as loyal."

I'd give anything to have my Martin pat my fanny as I wash up the supper dishes. Or have my ambitious Caroline hug my neck after I admire her work. Or have my sweet Charlotte crawl into my lap and beg for another song on the piano.

"Thank you for sticking it out, Polygon." Through tears, I look my bird in the eye. "Once I send Charlotte's new hire packing, we'll have our life back."

"Be nice." Polygon gives my finger a peck.

"Traitor." I recoil at his siding with Charlotte. "This has to be done, Polygon. And, no matter what anyone tries to tell me, I'm still the woman to do it."

BUY *Flying Fossils* @ **www.lynnegentry.com**

About the Author

Lynne Gentry knew marrying a pastor might change her plans. She didn't know how ministry would change her life. An author of numerous novels, short stories, and dramatic works, Lynne travels the country as a professional acting coach and inspirational speaker. Because Lynne's imagination loves to run wild, she also writes in the historical fiction genre of time travel and contemporary medical thrillers. You can come along on the adventures she takes into these other worlds at www.lynnegentry.com. She lives in Dallas with her husband and medical therapy dog. She counts spending time with her two grown children and their families her greatest joy.